Lust, Lies and Lemo

By Steven M

Special mention to Vicky.
To Michael Murphy for his excellent cover, to Karl Duke for his help with the original title. To Duke's cafe and The Wheatsheaf. Also to Emma, Liza, Lauren and Reece, for continuing to provide the inspiration.

For Kathleen and Arthur, my friends,
Family, and readers.

Sunday 11th May

There are certain moments in life when wishing the ground would open up and swallow you whole doesn't seem quite enough. Sometimes you deserve to be chewed up and spat out several times before you're eventually swallowed.

Moments such as when I inadvertently exposed myself to my son's teenage girlfriend, and realised she couldn't actually see anything because of my over-hanging stomach.

Or when the photograph my ever loving daughter took of my pyjama clad backside, sticking out of the wheelie bin, went viral on Facebook.

Or possibly when the woman who almost seduced me last night, arrived on my doorstep and introduced herself to my wife. Yes, most definitely the last one.

When Carol turned up at the door, I'd assumed it was to take her revenge for running out on her, and leaving her naked, alone, and with only four empty pizza boxes for company. Instead, she plonked herself down on the sofa and started telling us how she'd been in the area looking at renting a flat, when she suddenly remembered we lived close by and thought she'd call round and say hello.

Not that I believed a word of it mind you. Especially as she kept winking at me and running her tongue seductively over her upper lip stubble, whenever she thought Helen wasn't looking.

"Would you like another slice of lemon drizzle cake, Carol?" Asked Helen, when she noticed our guest had almost finished her first.

Carol eagerly rubbed her hands together. "Oh, yes please Helen." She said. "I can never say no to cake, no matter how many times I'm asked. Your husband will tell you that. We're always fighting over the last slice back at the taxi office. Isn't that right Eric?"

I didn't reply. I was too busy watching Helen for any signs of suspicion, as she picked up the now empty plate and headed through to the kitchen, throwing me a perplexed look as she went.

I knew exactly how she felt. Until Helen offered her the first slice I didn't even know we had any cake. I'd almost been tempted to follow her just to find out where she'd hidden it. Maybe she had a huge secret stash of other tasty delights somewhere that she and the children feasted upon whenever I'd left the house. I certainly wouldn't put it past them.

While all this was going on, neither was it helping my state of mind that since they arrived, my daughter and her new boyfriend, Timothy, the six foot ginger gorilla, had been in the back garden repeatedly kicking the football against the outside wall. It was bad enough having to entertain the woman I scorned, without having to worry about the windows being broken too.

I wouldn't have minded, but Sophie was only doing it to punish us for not letting her take her new beau upstairs to her bedroom.

"But why can't we go upstairs?" said Sophie, "It's not like we're going to be doing anything up there. I'm not stupid you know, dad."

"Maybe YOU'RE not stupid," I said, nodding towards the ginger gorilla, "But I know what boys are like. How old is he anyway? Are you sure you've not brought your boyfriend's dad round by mistake."

"I'm thirteen and three quarters," said Timothy, scratching one of his huge ginger sideburns.

Helen stared at him aghast. "Thirteen? You're only thirteen?"

I said, "Are you sure that's not in dog years?"

"People grow up a lot quicker now than they did in the olden day's dad," Said Sophie, with as much sarcasm as she could muster. "Can't we please just go up for five minutes then," She pleaded, "So I can show him my Wayne Rooney stuff?"

"No you bloody can't, I said firmly. "If he wants to look at any of the contents of your bedroom you can show him through the window. You're not having a boy in that room until you're at least eighteen."

Sophie pouted and folded her arms. "God this is so embarrassing. Well, if you're not going to let us go upstairs, I guess we'll just have to go outside and play football, wont we?" Then she grabbed hold of Timothy's arm and dragged him outside. Sticking her tongue out at me as she went.

And that was exactly where they spent the rest of the afternoon, repeatedly kicking the football against the outside wall, with the gorilla occasionally shouting "ROONEY," whenever he scored a goal.

Not that any of that really mattered. Not with the woman I almost accidentally slept with sitting opposite me in a low cut blouse, a completely inappropriate split skirt, crossing and uncrossing her legs, Sharon Stone style, whenever she caught me looking in her direction, and stuffing her face with my bloody cake.

As soon as Helen had left the room, I grabbed the opportunity and leaned in across the coffee table. "Look," I whispered, "I don't know what you're doing here Carol, but please, just go now before Helen starts to get suspicious."

Carol brushed some errant crumbs off her chest, making her huge boobs jiggle about beneath her blouse like a couple of over inflated bouncy castles. "I'll go when I'm ready thank you Eric. Unlike some people I'm not in the habit of sneaking out of people's houses as soon as they've gone into the kitchen. That would be just plain rude wouldn't it?"

Carol was obviously referring to last night, when I crept out of her flat, and she chased my car down the road wearing nothing but her knickers. Although the expression 'Least said soonest mended' probably wasn't intended for my wanton acts of yellow bellied cowardice, I decided it was probably best not to mention the incident anyway.

"Well, how about I just throw you out instead," I said, putting on my sternest and most masterful voice. "How would that be then?"

"And how do you intend on doing that?" She scoffed, "As far as I remember you had enough trouble trying to push me off your lap never mind anything else."

She was right. Unless it was under her own steam Carol was going nowhere. At least, not without the aid of a winch or a fork lift truck.

"What are you two talking about?" Helen had come back in and caught us whispering conspiratorially. "I hope Eric isn't trying to persuade you to give him a bite of your cake, Carol? He has told you he's on a diet hasn't he?"

"No, nothing like that. Eric was just saying that if I did move to the area, he'd be happy to help out with any decorating that I needed doing around the place."

Helen, who knows where DIY is concerned, she'd be better off asking Mr Bean to do it for her, raised an eyebrow. "What? Eric said that?"

"He did, and he offered to drive me home later." Carol took the plate from Helen and immediately began tucking in. "You know you've got yourself a heck of a good man there Helen. If he wasn't so happily married, I might even be after him myself." Then she threw back her head, and began guffawing so loudly I thought her cake was in danger of falling out of her mouth.

As I sat and watched Helen and Carol chatting away like a couple of old friends, accompanied by the occasional thud of a football bouncing off the outside wall, I began to wonder how I'd gotten myself into this predicament. It hadn't been that long ago Helen and I had been passionately kissing on the sofa, and on the verge of having sex for the first time since Father's day. Now I was on the verge of a nervous breakdown and about to drive the other woman back to her love nest instead. Talk about not having your cake, and not being able to eat the bloody thing either.

After almost thirty minutes of having to endure tantalising glimpses of Carol's thighs, as she crossed and uncrossed her legs at every available opportunity, I began to wonder whether she was ever going to leave. For the sake of my blood pressure, and probably my marriage, I decided to take matters into my own hands before it was too late.

"Are you ready to go then Carol? I said, taking a prolonged hard look at my watch, and then gesturing purposely towards the door, "We'd better be getting you home if we want to beat that traffic?"

Carol said, "It's six o'clock on a Sunday? There isn't any traffic. You wouldn't be trying to get rid of me by any chance would you Eric?"

I vigorously hoisted her up off the sofa. "Of course not," I said. "Why would I want to do something like that?"

It was obvious by the look she gave me Carol didn't entirely believe me, and judging by the way she was deliberately thrusting her backside against my groin as I tried to help her on with her jacket, she clearly wasn't going to leave without a fight.

My worries were doubly confirmed a moment later when Helen excused herself and took the dirty crockery through to the kitchen. No sooner was she through the door than Carol was on me, pushing me hard up against the wall.

I couldn't believe it. Not only was she brazenly rubbing her knee against my genitals, while my wife was in the next room, but one of her hands had snaked its way inside my shirt, and was busying itself trying to tune my left nipple into radio five.

All it would have taken at that moment was for my wife to walk back in and my marriage would have been done for. As I struggled to fend off Carol's advances, all I could see ahead of me was a future of loneliness, lawyers, and divorce courts, and Helen and I fighting over who would get custody of Sophie. The way my luck had been going lately, it would probably be me.

“Quick,” whispered Carol, “kiss me before she comes back.”

“No I bloody won’t,” I said. “Get your hands off me woman!”

“Oh come on Eric,” She said, rubbing her boobs against my midriff, “Don’t tell me you’ve forgotten about these already? You couldn’t get enough of them last night.”

I hadn’t forgotten them. Every time I closed my eyes, I could picture Carol whipping them out as she straddled me on her sofa. I doubt I’ll be able to block that memory out of my head, no matter how hard I try. For years after watching Alien, I’d wake up in a cold sweat after seeing that monster burst out of John Hurt’s chest. I’d imagine watching Carol’s breast’s exploding out of her bra, and then flopping down to my knees, would be equally difficult to forget.

Fortunately, just as I was beginning to feel my resolve weakening we heard Helen coming back and Carol moved quickly away again. Casually leaning against the sofa looking like the cat that got the cream, while I cowered breathlessly against the wall, praying my wife wouldn't notice my erect nipples.

“You alright, Eric?” Said Helen, looking me up and down. “Not coming down with something are you?”

I grinned inanely, “No, no I’m fine. Just a bit of a headache that’s all.”

And it was true, I had. If today had taught me anything, it was that lying through my back teeth, as well as my front teeth, really wasn't good for my health.

Back to Carol's

After Helen and Carol said their goodbyes, with Helen telling Carol, we really must get together more often, and Carol threatening to pop round anytime, now she knows where we are, I enthusiastically escorted Carol out through the front door, down to the car, and bundled her into the passenger seat.
Once round the corner and out of sight of the house, I pulled over to the side of the road.

"So, what was that all about?" I said, switching off the engine and turning towards her. "You have absolutely no intention of moving anywhere near here do you? You only came round to wind me up?"

"Oh, are we parking up," she asked, completely avoiding the question, "I haven't done that since I was a teenager. Do you want me in the back, or shall I climb over to you instead?"

I watched as Carol threw one leg over the other and twisted toward me in her seat, causing her already far too short skirt to ride up almost above the knicker line.

I groaned loudly as my eyes desperately tried not to look in the direction little Eric obviously wanted them to.

"You're just not listening Carol," I said. As little Eric eventually won out, and I found myself craning my neck forward for an even better view. "I don't want you anywhere near me. I'm sorry, but I'm just not interested anymore."

Carol ran her hand suggestively over the gear stick. "Try telling your eyes that Eric. If you can tear them away from my legs that is. You want me and you know it. You just won't admit it to yourself."

Carol was right. After last nights near miss at her flat, and this afternoon's almost moment with Helen, little Eric was feeling even less choosy who he performed a salute for than usual, but no matter how much I wanted Carol as I stared down at her blotchy red thighs, with just a tantalising glimpse of black knicker elastic, poking through the split in her skirt, I knew I had to resist.

I turned away and tried to find something less arousing to focus on. I looked down and there was an empty snickers wrapper poking out of the driver's door compartment. It was the one I'd devoured a couple of weeks earlier just before my first excursion on the exercise bike.

As my eyes focused on it in the late afternoon gloom, I noticed a piece of nutty chocolate in the corner I must have forgotten to lick off. I was having such a bad day I was almost tempted to reach down and finish it right then, but the last thing I needed was to show Carol any signs of weakness, no matter how deliciously tempting it looked. Instead, I tried to concentrate on the matter at hand.

"I'm sorry Carol," I said solemnly. "I'm sorry if I hurt you. I'm sorry for leading you on, but I love Helen. I've always loved Helen, and I always will. I'm sorry, but you and me, it's just never going to happen."

Carol was silent, and for a brief moment I thought I'd managed to get through to her. At least I did until I heard her yelp, "Look, there's a Snickers wrapper down there, and it's still got some chocolate in it." Then she was suddenly leaning over me, her monumental boobs squashed into my groin as she reached across and grabbed it.

I watched Carol pop it in her mouth and avidly tongue the wrapper as she tried to lick off every last morsel and I realised I'd absolutely made the right decision. She hadn't even offered to share it.

Carol noticed me staring at her. "What's wrong with you? Waste not, want not. Isn't that the way it goes?"

I shook my head. "Yes, but you've just eaten two slices of lemon cake?"

"Oh, that was ages ago," she said, scrunching up the wrapper and leaning back in her seat, "And in answer to your question, yes, I did just come round to wind you up. Now take me home please. I think we've both had enough fun for one afternoon."

When I parked up outside Carol's flat, I really didn't know what to say. I'd already done my best to apologise, but whether she'd accepted it or not I still had no idea. Carol had admitted she'd only come round to annoy me, but was that the end of it or was she likely to keep turning up on my doorstep whenever she wanted to watch me squirm?

"So, are we ok now Carol?" I asked hopefully, my eyes searching hers for some sign she was ready to forgive me.

Carol put her finger to her mouth and thought for a moment. "Hmm, are we ok?" She said, unbuckling her seatbelt, "Well, let's see if this answers your question." Then she grabbed hold of my jacket, pulled me towards her, and clamped her mouth firmly over mine.

It was only a brief kiss, but in the short time it took for Carol's Snickers flavoured tongue to force itself between my lips, and suck mine back between hers, I began to realise exactly how a carpet must feel when it's being vacuumed by a Dyson. However, just as I came to my senses, and tried to extricate my tongue from the vice-like grip of Carol's mouth, I felt her hands on my chest as she suddenly pushed me away again.

"You know you really hurt me last night," She said, wiping the drool from her mouth, with the back of her hand. "Do you have any idea how embarrassing it is running down the road in just your knickers? Having strangers pointing at you in the street? Having little kids shouting fatty fatty bum bum at you, and the older ones shouting show us your tits?"

“Sorry,” I whispered, looking down towards my feet, trying to look suitably apologetic. “It must have been awful for you.”

“Awful isn’t the word Eric. I doubt I’ll ever be able to look any of my neighbours in the eye ever again. So in answer to your question – well, I guess we’ll just have to see, won't we.” Then she looked at me smiled. Not an everyday kind of smile. More the type of smile Bernard Matthews might have given a turkey when he was approaching it with a carving knife.

As I watched Carol climb out of the car and totter along the pavement, her buttocks swinging provocatively beneath her too tight skirt as she went, I suddenly felt the overwhelming urge for a McDonalds. After the day I’d had, not only was I desperately in need of some comfort food, but after witnessing Carol devour my cake, and tongue what remained of my Snickers bar, I was feeling positively ravenous. So on the way home I treated myself to two cheeseburgers, large fries, and a strawberry shake.

I was sitting in the car park finishing the last of the fries and the burgers when I received a text from Carol. The message read: ‘Just in case you didn’t get a good enough look earlier,’ and was accompanied by a photograph of her lacy black knickers. The woman really does have no shame. She hadn’t even bothered to take them off first.

The last thing I wanted to do was give her any encouragement so I didn’t reply. Although it was kind of flattering being in the sights of a sexual predator like Carol, considering what she’d just told me, it was also becoming increasingly unnerving. If the last couple of days had taught me anything, it was how much I loved Helen and if things continue the way they are I'm in serious danger of losing her. Especially if Carol kept taking it upon herself to turn up on my doorstep whenever the fancy took her. My nerves are bad enough as it is, without that playing on my mind too.

Once I'd finished eating I scrolled through my phone and deleted every text, photograph, and Facebook message Carol has ever sent me, then drove back home to my wife.

Back home

After earlier being interrupted by Carol, Sophie, and the six foot ginger gorilla, I wasn't feeling particularly hopeful that Helen would still be in the mood by the time I got back. Especially as it wasn't a leap year. However when I opened the door I was amazed to find, '*I Want You Back for Good,*' by Take That, blasting out of the stereo.

Helen's always had a huge crush on Gary Barlow, and often listens to his music whenever she's feeling frisky. I even offered to take her to a concert during our sex embargo, in the hope that it might reignite her fires. Unfortunately the tickets sold out in about forty two seconds, and I wasn't about to pay nearly a grand to a ticket tout. Not even if it did guarantee a well overdue leg-over.

"That you Eric?" I heard Helen yell from upstairs. "I'm in the bedroom. There's some wine in the kitchen. Why don't you bring it up with you?"

I couldn't believe it. It looked like Helen and I were about to have sex and it wasn't even a special occasion. At least I didn't think it was? After checking the calendar to make sure today's date hadn't been circled as a birthday or anniversary, I grabbed the wine and glasses and sprinted up the stairs. I was moving so quickly I must have worked off the calories of a cheeseburger before I'd even reached the landing.

Once I'd reached the top of the stairs, I stopped and gathered myself. First, I checked my face in the bathroom mirror for any incriminating signs of Carol's lipstick that may have inadvertently, or possibly deliberately, been left behind, then my armpits for any undesirable smells. I probably could have done with a shower, but Helen was so rarely in the mood these days, the last thing I wanted to do was give her a chance to go off the boil again. Thinking on my feet I sprayed some Lynx under my armpits and inside my underpants, undid the top two buttons of my shirt, and swaggered sexily into the bedroom.

Diary, after so many months of celibacy Helen really was a sight to behold. She lay on the bed in a red see through negligee, nothing else, just the negligee. Even though the lights were off and the blinds were shut, I was pretty sure she'd even taken the trouble to give her cat a bit of a trim too.

I put the wine and the glasses on the bedside table as I drank my wife in. "Helen, you look wonderful."

She said, "Well, that was the intention."

"Sophie?"

She's gone out with Timothy. I know its school tomorrow but I thought this was more important, so I gave her twenty pounds, and told her not to come back until at least eight o clock."

I sat on the bed and started pulling off my socks. "I'm not sure I like the idea of Sophie having a boyfriend," I said. "Especially one who looks even older than I do. Do you think we should ask to see some ID?"

Helen scooted up behind me and wrapped her arms around my shoulders. "Forget about Sophie, At least for a few hours anyway. Tonight's about you and me."

As I turned my head towards Helen, her lips were quickly on mine, and moments later we were kissing deeply and passionately, as we fell backwards onto the bed.
I remember thinking, *'This is my third snog of the day and it hadn't even gone dark yet. I doubt even Andrew or Next door's cat could beat a record like that.'*

Unfortunately diary, it didn't take long for me to realise something wasn't quite right. I was lying on my back enjoying the warmth of Helen's body against mine as we kissed and stroked each other, when I suddenly realised little Eric was still fast asleep. Talk about bad timing. He'd been wide awake and performing salutes here, there, and everywhere, throughout the rest of the day, but now I really needed him, he'd gone and slipped into a coma.

I tried to concentrate on the moment, running my hands all over Helen's incredibly sexy body as I willed the little guy to come out to play, but no matter what I did, or where I fondled, little Eric was having none of it.

As our kissing continued I felt Helen's hand moving downwards so I grabbed it and pulled it to my chest. Hoping if I gave him just a few more minutes he'd suddenly spring to life.

After all, he'd had a pretty exhausting day so far. What with snogging Helen on the sofa, Carol's knickers, and then being tongued in the car. He was probably getting a bit fed up of loading up his rifle and running out of the barracks only to realise he wasn't going into battle after all. Maybe he just needed a few minutes to realise what was going on before he leapt into action again.

I was wrong. After I pulled Helen's hand away for the fourth time she stopped kissing me and blinked several times. "Eric, I know it's been a while, but even you must remember that when you have sex it's much easier if you take your trousers off first?"

Stalling for time, I told Helen I wanted to enjoy being close to her before we moved onto the main event. Then I suggested we just kiss for a while and get to know each other again. I could tell Helen didn't really want to wait, but I didn't know what else to do.

"Are you sure?" She said, "Sophie won't be gone for that long you know?"

"Don't worry. It won't take me long once we get going."

"Yes, I remember," She sighed, "Well, ok, if that's what you want?"

For the next twenty minutes Helen and I lay on the bed snogging like a couple of teenagers but still there was nothing. As I felt Helen's hand moving towards him for the fifth time I reached out and pulled it back to my chest again.

"Right that's it," said Helen sitting up, "What the hell's going on? I thought this was what you wanted?"

"It is," I said, "It really is."

"Well then, stop mucking about and get those bloody pants off. We haven't got all night you know, Eric."

I pulled myself away from Helen and swung my legs over the side of the bed. The last thing I wanted to do was tell my wife little Eric appeared to have lost interest in her, but it didn't look like I had any other option.

"I really don't understand this," said Helen, who had climbed off the bed and was now pacing about the room. "One minute you're all over me and the next you don't even want to get undressed? I have seen it all before you know, Eric. I mean, what the hell is wrong with you?" Helen suddenly stopped talking and stood over me gazing down at my crotch. At first I thought it was because she'd finally noticed the lack of any kind of tent in my trousers. But then she pointed towards my nether region and blinked several times. "Wait a minute. This isn't because you're wearing dirty underwear again is it Eric? Because if it is..."

I was about to interrupt her and say, no it bloody isn't, when it suddenly occurred to me Helen had inadvertently handed me a ready-made excuse on a plate. There was no way my wife would want to sleep with me if she thought I was wearing filthy Y fronts. No matter how randy she was feeling.

Looking up I swallowed what was left of my pride and nodded. "Sorry Helen. I think it's all this healthy food I've been eating. I always said Ryvitas and organic vegetables couldn't be good for you."

I watched in silence as Helen began pulling on her nightgown. "Well in that case why don't we leave it for tonight? *Coronation Street* will be starting soon, and to be honest, the mood's kind of gone off me."

I didn't want the night to end like that, but I didn't have any other options. For whatever reason my penis had decided to go on strike, and was absolutely refusing to break the picket line. But that really wasn't something I wanted to share with Helen.

"Well, if you're sure that's what you want," I said.

Helen nodded, "I think it's for the best. I might even get the bike out for an hour and work off some of this excess energy." Then she grabbed her exercise gear out of the drawer, and stomped off to the bathroom.

Diary, judging by how much energy Helen had to burn off I've obviously just missed the best night's sex since our honeymoon. Two bloody hours she spent pedalling away like a lunatic. She pedalled away through the entirety of *Coronation Street*, and until at least the fifth death in *Midsomer Murders*. At one point her feet were a blur, and the wheels were making so much noise I had to turn up the TV, so I could hear who Inspector Barnaby was accusing of murdering the vicar with a cricket bat. Why couldn't my penis have picked another night to decide to go to bed early?

Hopefully by tomorrow he'll have had a good night's rest, and Helen and I will finally be able to get our marriage back on track.

Monday 12th May

When I woke up this morning I thought everything was back to normal. Little Eric was up and about and desperate for a wee, even before the alarm clock had gone off. However, as I lay in bed watching Helen towelling herself dry, and getting dressed after her shower, he suddenly decided to go back to sleep again.

That really isn't right. Even the thought of a wet and naked Helen used to have him raiding the armoury in case he was called into action. As soon as he saw her this morning he decided to desert.

I was so worried I waited until Sophie had left for school and Helen had left for work, then downloaded last week's episodes of *Hollyoaks*, to see if he'd give the response he usually does.

Normally, while watching *Hollyoaks*, there'd be so many Mexican waves going on in my underpants I'd be worried about the elastic snapping. This time, however, although he briefly popped up to wave hello, as soon as my mind drifted back to Helen he disappeared back into his shell again.

I really don't know what the hell's going on. I did a search on my laptop, and the best answer it could come up with was, I'm either depressed, anxious, or suffering from possible relationship issues. The way my luck's been going it's probably all three.

The whole situation with Carol isn't helping either. Even as I was googling my symptoms, she sent me a text letting me know she was thinking of me accompanied by a winking smiley face.

When Carol was thinking of me last week I'd probably have been naked, but after what she told me in my taxi I dread to think what she's imagining now? I certainly wouldn't have been surprised if my genitals and a meat grinder were involved somewhere along the line.

As when I woke up, little Eric's condition proved it's not a physical issue, I've decided to ignore it for now. A couple of weeks ago there was a loud clanking noise coming from under my car bonnet, but before I had a chance to get to the garage it suddenly stopped on its own anyway. Maybe the ignoring and hoping for the best repair method, will be just as effective with my genitals too.

Tuesday 13th May

I'm beginning to suspect next doors fat ginger tom is spreading the word around the neighbourhood about my garden being a public cat toilet. As it was a nice day, I thought I'd do a bit of gardening to take my mind off my troubles, but it seemed like every time I stuck the trowel in the ground it came back out again covered in cat crap. The borders were absolutely full of it. By the time I'd finished, it was almost overflowing my bucket. At first I thought the fat ginger tom must be burying them over a long period of time, but judging by the different shapes and sizes, there's no way they could all belong to the same bloody cat. No matter how proficient its bottom was.

I was so annoyed that when I saw Abigail the emo on the way to the shed to visit Andrew, I handed her the bucket and told her to give it to her dad. She didn't really know what to say when I left her standing in the middle of the garden, holding her nose in the air, as she held the bucket at arm's length, but I don't see why I should be the only one to get my bloody hands dirty.

Wednesday 14th May

Logged on to Facebook and discovered that Sophie is now officially in a relationship with Timothy, the six foot ginger gorilla. The status had only been up forty minutes, but it already had over a hundred likes. Even Helen and Andrew had given them a cyber thumbs up. I did think about reporting it as spam, but if Sophie had found out I doubt she'd ever forgive me.

While logged on, I took the opportunity to take a look at Timothy's profile. Diary, despite being nearly six feet tall and badly in need of a shave, it seems he really is only thirteen years old. Not only that, but his timeline seemed to have more pictures of Wayne Rooney than Sophie's and Melody's put together. It's no wonder Sophie's keen on him. He seems to fancy Wayne even more than she does.

Thursday 15th May

Received a Facebook message from my next door neighbour Ron. The message read:

Dear Eric,

Although I'm grateful for your very generous gift, I can't help wondering why you felt I was in need of a bucket full of cat shit? While I do appreciate we all need a hobby. Rest assured the collecting of feline faeces is one interest of yours I have absolutely no intention of becoming involved in.
However, as an extra bucket will always come in handy, I've returned the contents to your side of the fence and given the bucket a very thorough wash.

Your neighbour and friend, Ron.

I sent the following reply:

Dear Ron,

Allow me to apologise. I handed the bucket to Abigail, while I went into the house to fetch a black bin liner to put the contents in to. I can only assume Abigail mistook the word 'bag' for 'dad' and gave it to you instead. Therefore, if you could return my bucket at your earliest convenience, I would of course, be most extremely grateful.

Your neighbour and friend, Eric.

A few minutes later I received the following response.

A completely understandable mistake to make Eric. Especially if Abigail had recently been listening to Andrew playing his music, and had forgotten to remove her ear plugs.

After scooping up all the cat dung and putting it in a black bin liner, I waited until all the lights had gone off next door, sneaked down the side of the house, and dropped it in Ron's bin. I don't see why I should have to keep polluting my wheelie bin especially when it isn't even my bloody cat.

Friday 16th May

Just watched *Fatal Attraction* with Helen. I didn't want to but apparently it's the first offering of Sky movies, wronged women out for revenge season, and Helen has never seen it before.

I may not have slept with Carol, but it was still rather worrying watching Glenn Close stalk Michael Douglas as she sought to pay him back for his wrongdoings. Particularly the part where she tried to murder Michael with a kitchen knife?

Although I'm fairly certain Carol isn't a homicidal maniac, they do say that hell hath no fury like a woman scorned.

I can only hope that if Carol does turn up looking for a pet to put in the pot, next doors cat is taking a shit in my garden at the time.

As Little Eric was still away on holiday, I was also becoming concerned the films raunchy action may have put Helen in the mood for a spontaneous night of love action. Fortunately, although Helen did suddenly lunge towards me during one particularly sexy scene, it was only to pinch one of my Ryvitas.

A few weeks ago that would have disappointed me. This time, all I did was breathe a huge sigh of relief. Especially as I can't bloody stand Ryvitas.

Saturday 17th May

As Helen and I were still in Sophie's bad books since refusing bedroom admission to her ginger boyfriend, we decided to take her and her best friend Melody out for tea. Sophie may be even more stubborn than her mother, but she's usually a lot more forgiving and agreeable once you stick a fourteen inch pepperoni pizza down in front of her.

I'd been looking forward to a pizza myself, but as I was reading the menu, Sophie said, "I hope you're not having a pizza dad? Do you know how many calories are in one of those?"

I said, "I'm sure it doesn't matter for one night," but after Melody helpfully Googled how fattening their smallest pizza was, I begrudgingly had a low fat cheese and ham jacket potato instead.

Diary, it was awful. Watching the three of them cramming their faces with, between them, over forty inches of pizza and a couple of feet of garlic bread, while I picked at my potato.

Neither does it help that when you're overweight and eating low calorie food, you can't help feeling that everyone in the place, particularly the staff, are aware that you're on a diet. The waitress didn't even ask who the potato was for. She put it down in front of me, smiled sympathetically, and said, "I'm guessing this is for you sir?"

While we were eating all Sophie could talk about was Timothy. She was telling us what subjects he was taking at school, what music he was into, what his parents were like, and how much he loved Wayne bloody Rooney. She was going on about him so much even Melody started to look a bit bored. To try and change the subject, Helen asked Melody if she had a boyfriend yet.

"God, no," She said, "I wouldn't let a boy anywhere near me."

"I bet your dad's pleased about that," I said, throwing a sideways glance at my daughter. "You see Sophie. Why couldn't you be more like Melody?"

Sophie said, "Dad, I wish you'd stop going on about it. I haven't even let him kiss me yet."

I said, "Good. As long as it stays that way then we won't have to lock you in your bedroom until you go away to university."

Sophie shook her head, "You know you're such a hypocrite dad. You didn't treat Andrew like this when he started dating Abby, and you know why? It's because he's got a penis, and I haven't. I bet if I had something pink and wrinkled dangling between my legs you wouldn't care whether I was dating or not."

I said, "It wouldn't make any difference. It's because Andrew's seventeen and you've only just turned thirteen. It only seems five minutes ago you were playing with dolls and bringing home buckets of frogspawn, and now you're bringing home spotty teenage boys instead."

"I've never touched frogspawn in my life," Exclaimed Sophie. "And Timothy is not spotty!"

"No, he isn't," I said. "I'm not sure he's a boy either. Have you seen the size of his Adams apple? When I first saw him I thought he was trying to swallow a coconut."

Sophie bit into a piece of garlic bread. "I don't know why you're worried anyway dad. It's not like I'm going to get into trouble or anything. I don't think I can, now that mum's put me on the pill."

Diary, it's a good job I didn't have pizza, because if I'd been eating anything other than a tiny piece of potato, I probably would have choked to death. Not that anybody would have cared. There I was, red faced and gasping for breath and not one person in the restaurant even offered to help. You'd have thought someone might have rushed over to slap me on the back, or perform the Heimlich manoeuvre, but apart from the woman at the next table who kept turning round and tutting very loudly, they all just carried on eating.

Even Helen wasn't very sympathetic. When I finally did manage to dislodge the piece of potato from my throat, and bring my coughing under control, all she could say was, "Oh, for pity's sake Eric, Stop making a scene."

"Making a scene?" I spluttered, "I thought I was choking to death. Have you heard what she's just said?"

"Oh, don't be so melodramatic. How long have you known our daughter for? You must know she's only winding you up."

Sophie said, "Well derr. No need to have a heart attack dad."

"Now, can we please leave it," said Helen. "I'm sure Melody doesn't want to sit here listening to you two squabble all night."

"I don't mind," said Melody.

Helen snarled, "Well, I do mind. Let's just sit here quietly and try and enjoy our food."

And that's precisely what we did. For the next thirty minutes we all sat in stony silence, as Helen and the girls finished there pizzas and I ate my potato.

The atmosphere still wasn't much better by the time we arrived home. Sophie ran straight upstairs to her bedroom, leaving Melody to say, "Thanks for my tea, Mr and Mrs Baxter," before scampering after her.

I took off my jacket as Helen glared at me with her hands on her hips. "Well, as bridge building exercises go Eric," she eventually said, "I'd have to say, it probably wasn't the most successful night ever."

I said, "I know. I'm sorry, I just don't like the idea of Sophie having a boyfriend."

"And you think I do? But this is Sophie we're talking about. If a boy even tried touching her, he'd probably go home wearing his testicles as ear muffs. I can't think of anyone less likely than our daughter to do anything stupid, can you?"

I knew Helen was right, but it wasn't going to stop me worrying. When I was a thirteen year old boy, aside from football and action men, girls were pretty much all I thought about. True, the only thing they ever thought about me was that they wouldn't touch me with a ten foot barge pole, but that didn't stop me trying. If Timothy was anything like every other teenage boy that had ever lived, I was pretty sure it wouldn't stop him giving it a go either.

Of course it didn't help that Sophie was growing up to look just like her mother. She had the same eyes, the same smile, and if anything was becoming even more beautiful and alluring than Helen ever was. Why couldn't she be more like me? I know from personal experience, if Sophie was growing up with my looks and personality I wouldn't have to worry about the opposite sex wanting to go anywhere near her, until she was at least ten years out of puberty.

10.05pm

After running Melody home, I texted Helen to tell her I was calling into the office, then went for a pizza.
I had a twelve inch chicken, mushroom, and jalapeno and four slices of garlic bread.

Although I did feel slightly guilty, I must admit, it was still quite rewarding sitting back at the same table, as the waitress from earlier fetched my order.

"Yes, it is all for me," I said, grinning broadly, as a look of recognition spread across her face, "and I intend to eat every last morsel, thank you very much."

It may not have done much for my waistline, but it was certainly a lot less embarrassing than ordering another potato.

Sunday 18th May

Timothy came to visit Sophie today. Helen, and I didn't even know he was coming until he turned up at the door, carrying his football, and a fistful of dandelions. "Hello Mr and Mrs Baxter," he grunted, "Is Sophie coming out?"

I wanted to say, no she bloody isn't, and why have you brought my daughter a bunch of flowers that according to folklore are supposed to make her wet the bed. But as I stared at his huge cockeyed grin, Helen suddenly pushed me out of the way, and said, "Don't just stand there looking gormless Eric. Invite the poor boy in."

I sometimes wonder why I bother trying to be the master in this house. I'm even further down the pecking order than next door's cat.

Timothy wanted to go out, but because Sophie knew it would annoy me, she decided to hang around the house all afternoon. Then, just in case that wasn't enough, she then insisted he stay for his tea too.

What Sophie didn't realise was, although it was frustrating seeing them together it was much more preferable to not having a clue where they were, or more importantly, what they were up to. At least while she was following me around the house I knew she wasn't busy fighting off Timothy's advances behind some bushes somewhere. Keeping an eye on them was relatively simple, when I knew that no matter where I went Sophie would appear moments later, dragging Timothy along behind her.

If I was in the dining room Sophie would come in so she could show Timothy the exercise bike she'd suddenly developed a keen interest in. If I was in the kitchen, she'd follow me to see if we had any chocolate digestives left in the biscuit tin. Even though thanks to my diet, she already knew we bloody hadn't.

The only place she didn't try to follow me was the bathroom. Even Sophie wasn't stubborn enough to go in there after me. In the end I gave up and settled in the lounge with a Ryvita and a cup of tea.

"We're just going to come in and watch some television," said Sophie, as she and Timothy plonked themselves down either side of me on the sofa. "You don't mind, do you dad?"

"Why would I mind," I said. "You know spending quality time with my daughter makes my life all the more worthwhile."

I didn't look, but I was pretty certain Sophie was sticking her tongue out at me when I said that. Call it Father's instinct if you will.

"Well, this is nice," said Helen, when she came in and saw us all scrunched up awkwardly together on the sofa, "Can I get anybody anything from the kitchen? Sophie? Timothy? Would anybody like anything to drink? I think we've got some lemonade in the cupboard? What about something to eat? I think we've still got some ham and cheese in the fridge. I don't mind making some sandwiches, if anybody's hungry?"

I couldn't believe it. For some reason Helen had suddenly turned into Mary Poppins. Anybody would think she wanted Sophie to have a boyfriend, the way she was carrying on.

“No mum, we’re fine,” Said Sophie, “Will you please just stop fussing about.”

“Sorry,” said Helen. “I just wondered if anybody was hungry, that’s all. Your tea won’t be ready for a few hours yet.”

“Well, we’re not mum. We’re both fine,” snapped Sophie.

Helen mouthed the word sorry again, and plopped herself down in the armchair. I couldn’t help smiling. If nothing else it certainly made a nice change to be the least embarrassing parent for once.

After a few minutes of pretending to read one of her magazines, Helen then decided to make matters worse, by inexplicably trying to strike up a conversation with the gorilla. “So Timothy,” she said brightly, “You like football, do you?”

“Yes, Mrs Baxter.”

“I thought so,” She said. “Every time I see you you’ve got one of your balls in your hand.”

Even now I don’t know how I managed to stop myself from spurting my tea everywhere.

Sophie leapt to her feet. “Right that’s it! I didn’t invite Timothy over so you could ask him stupid questions mum.”

"What have I done now? All I did was ask if he liked playing football?"

"It's not what you said mum, it's the way you said it. Honestly, you're just so embarrassing sometimes."

"Oh, well, pardon me for breathing. I'll try to say things the correct way in future."

"You can say what you like," Said Sophie. "We're going to play football until tea's ready." Then she flounced out of the room dragging a bewildered looking Timothy along behind her. I've often thought that if flouncing were an Olympic event, our daughter would be breaking even more records than Usain Bolt.

As soon as they'd gone I turned toward my wife. "Well Helen, I said, "As bridge building exercises go, that probably wasn't your most successful afternoon ever."

"Oh, shut up Eric."

The rest of the day went by relatively quietly. After trying unsuccessfully to watch the afternoon film, while listening to Timothy's football pounding against the wall, Helen dragged me upstairs to help her change the bedding. As Helen took another load down to the washing machine, I realised I couldn't hear the ball anymore, so I went into Sophie's room and peeked out of the window.

I'm not really sure what I expected to see when I climbed on her chest of drawers and stared down into the garden, but it was actually rather sweet. Sophie and Timothy were sitting cross-legged on the grass, rolling the ball to each other as they laughed and chatted away in the afternoon sunshine. It certainly looked very innocent. If anything, it reminded me of Helen and I when we first started seeing each other. Especially when they got up and Timothy tried to put his arm around her waist, and Sophie pushed him away with so much force, he staggered backwards across the lawn until he fell flat on his backside.

Sophie really is growing up to be just like her mother. And I for one, couldn't be more proud.

After we'd finished eating, I volunteered to do the washing up. The bin bag was full so I changed it and took it outside to the wheelie bin. When I was coming back inside I noticed Timothy's football, just lying there on the lawn, completely unattended.

Diary, I really didn't mean to. Call it a moment of madness if you will. But once I'd checked to make sure nobody was looking, I picked up the ball and hid it at the bottom of the wheelie bin.

I did feel slightly guilty when Timothy's bottom lip started to wobble because he thought it had been stolen, but better that I thought than listening to the bloody thing bouncing off the wall again while I'm trying to watch television. Besides, I'll probably have fished it back out again before the bin men come.

Monday 19th May

Helen made another play for me tonight. At least I assumed that was what she was doing. I can't think of any other reason why she'd suddenly start whispering my name and stroking my nipples during the middle of the night.

To make matters worse, I was having a really nice dream until she interrupted. I dreamt I was attending the final of The Great British Bake off. Just as the competition was about to begin, Paul Hollywood was taken ill and Mary Berry asked if a member of the audience would be willing to volunteer as a guest judge. Never being one to shirk my responsibilities, I immediately climbed over the hoarding and offered my assistance. However, just as I was about to sink my teeth into the first contestants rather delicious looking double chocolate gateau, I could feel Helen's little finger slowly circling my nipple through my pyjama top.

Talk about bad bloody timing. Unfortunately for me, Helen's sexual urges have obviously become like buses. You wait months for one to turn up then two suddenly arrive in quick succession.

"Are you awake, Eric?" She whispered.

What I wanted to say was, yes I am, throw back the duvet, and ravish my wife until the sun came up, but even as I felt Helen's hand trying to undo my top button, I knew it would be a waste of time. Helen may have succeeded in arousing me, but my penis was still out for the count.

Rather than admit the truth, I did the only thing I could do under those circumstances. I pretended to snore, pushed Helen's hand away, and rolled away towards the edge of the bed.

Diary, although I couldn't see my wife's face I could sense her disappointment. Especially when she muttered, “I'll take that as a no, then.”

As I lay in the dark, listening to Helen's rhythmic breathing as she slowly drifted back to sleep, I knew I couldn't let things carry on as they are. Just over a week ago even the mere thought of Helen trying to unbutton my pyjama top would have had little Eric leaping about in my underpants like a jack in the box. These days, unless I reach down and the have the occasional rummage about, I wouldn't even know he was still in there, never mind anything else.

When I did manage to fall back asleep again, I dreamt I was playing football in the garden with Sophie and Timothy. Sophie made me play in goal, but because they couldn’t find the football anywhere they were kicking cat turds at me instead. Diary, there were bloody hundreds of them. And as I’d suddenly turned into the greatest goalkeeper in the world, I managed to save every single shot. I was catching them, I was clutching them to my chest, I even headed quite a few of the bigger ones over the crossbar. Then every time I thought they’d run out of turds, a grinning Ron would suddenly appear and drop another huge bucketful over the fence. “There you go, Eric,” He’d say. “Plenty more where they came from.” Why couldn’t Helen have woken me up from that bloody dream?

I hate to admit it, but no matter how much I try I doubt I'll ever dream I was a guest judge on the Great British Bake Off ever again.

Tuesday 20th May

When the house was empty, I went into the garden to get Timothy’s football out of the wheelie bin. As I almost suffocated to death the last time I tried to retrieve something from the bottom of the bin, I decided to be sensible this time, and emptied the contents out onto the pavement. It may have been a lot messier, but it was definitely a lot less life threatening.

As I was in the kitchen rinsing the ball under the tap, I received a picture message from Carol. In the photo she was leaning back in a leather chair with her blouse open to the waist. The message read, just wanted to say thank you for the other night, and if you ever fancy getting your hands on these puppies ever again, feel free to pop round anytime you like.

I couldn’t believe it. How on Earth she had the nerve to call those breasts puppies was beyond me. If anything they were more like a couple of Great Danes.

Not only that, but judging by the radio in the background she'd clearly taken the photo while working in the cab office. I can only hope there weren't any drivers in at the time. Knowing Carol, she probably have asked one of them to take it.

I knew it was wrong, but as the house was empty, and there'd barely been a sighting of little Eric since last Sunday, I decided to use Carol's photo to see if I could persuade him to put in an appearance. I locked all the doors and windows, closed the blinds and tried to pummel the little guy into submission.

I must have spent a good fifteen minutes imagining Carol in various states of wantonness but no matter what images I conjured up, I could barely raise a smile, never mind anything else.

At one point, I was so frustrated, I was standing in the middle of the lounge with my underwear round my ankles, yelling, "What the bloody hell's wrong with you? Work, God dam you, work!"

I must have been shouting far too loudly, because as I was reaching down to pull up my trousers the head of next door's fat ginger tom poked itself through the blinds and glared at me across the room.

In my haste to lock up, I'd closed the window but forgot to put the catch on. The cat must have been lurking on the outside window ledge waiting for just the right moment to catch me at my most vulnerable.

As I shuffled towards it with my arms outstretched like some kind of half-naked penguin, I twisted my foot in the trouser leg, staggered into the coffee table, and finished up lying flat on my naked backside in the middle of the living room carpet.

Diary, I swear that after looking me up and down, that cat shook its head in disdain, gave a snort of contempt, before meowing, and pulling its head back out through the blinds.

I really need to sort myself out. It's coming to something when even next door's cat is starting to feel sorry for me.

Wednesday 21st May

Helen was cycling away her frustrations on the exercise bike again today. Not only did she cycle away through Neighbours and Home and Away but she refused to stop until Emmerdale had finished. She was going so fast that when she did eventually take her feet off the pedals, it took a good five minutes for the wheels to stop spinning.

Judging by how much energy she had to burn if we had slept together last night, I probably would've had to take a week off work just to recuperate.

"Wow, I really needed that," she said, wiping the sweat from her forehead before heading up for a shower. "It's good to blow off a little steam now and again, don't you think, Eric?"

I wasn't entirely certain but I'm sure I could detect a little sarcasm in Helen's voice when she said the word, Eric. I could definitely detect some when she said the words 'blow off'.

I really wish things were different. Helen was looking so sexy right then, dripping with sweat in her skin tight leggings and vest, that if I'd been capable I'd have ran upstairs and joined her in the shower to let off a little steam of my own. However because of my predicament I watched *Eastenders* with Sophie instead. Somehow diary, it wasn't quite the same.

Thursday 22nd May

Thought I saw Carol earlier. I was on the late shift and it was pitch black by the time I arrived home. As I turned into our street my headlights swept past a large shadowy figure standing at the bottom of the garden staring up at the house. After watching Fatal Attraction the other night my first thoughts were Carol was about to run amok and murder every member of the household, but when I got out of the car and rushed towards her the figure turned out to be nothing more sinister than our black wheelie bin with a bag dumped on top. I'd forgotten it was bin collection day.

Diary, I can only assume that I'm so hungry I'm starting to hallucinate. Given how constantly hungry I am it's a pity I couldn't imagine a chip butty instead.

Besides practically starving to death, it also isn't helping my mood, that despite my best efforts there's still no sign of little Eric. If you exclude first thing in the morning when I'm desperate for a wee, my genitals haven't spent this long out of action since before I hit puberty.

Friday 23rd May

Rang the doctor's first thing, hoping to see someone about my problem. By the time I managed to get through to reception I was told all the appointments had gone for the day and I'd have to try again on Monday. It's a good job I'm not seriously ill. If I were suffering from anything apart from erection problems I'd probably be dead by then.

I asked if it were possible to book an appointment for next week, while I was already on the phone to them, to save me ringing back. The receptionist said, "Are you a psychic, Mr Baxter?"

I said, "Well of course I'm not a bloody psychic."

She said, "Well, if you're not a psychic how on Earth do you know if you're going to be ill next week? You might wake up on Monday feeling right as rain and then you'll have taken up the appointment of someone who really is ill. Doctors valuable time is not to be wasted on frivolities, Mr Baxter."

“I said, “Look, I’m not ill and I’m not planning to be ill. I just want to see the doctor regarding a personal matter. Is that really such a difficult task to accomplish?”

She said, “Well, if it wasn’t I wouldn’t be doing my job properly.”

After much toing and froing the receptionist did tell me I could ring later in the day to see if there'd been any cancellations, but I decided to leave it for the moment. Chances are, I'm worrying about nothing and things will put themselves right anyway. In fact, the way my luck's been running lately, if I had got an appointment, I wouldn't have been surprised if I suddenly sprouted an erection while the doctor was examining it.

Saturday 24th May

Had a battle of wits with a pigeon on my way to pick up a fare this morning. Normally when I see a bird in the road I’m quietly confident it will have flown off by the time my car gets there. But as I was speeding towards this one, it seemed completely unaware it was about to get run over and just carried on strutting about like it was king of the bloody road.

Refusing to be beaten by a bird, I backed up and sped towards it while flashing my headlights, hoping to scare it away. Only to be forced to slam on the brakes again as it stood defiantly in the middle of the road, cooing, and bobbing its cocky little pigeon head about.

I did think about turning around and going the other way, but there was no way I was going to be bullied by a pigeon. It was bad enough having to put up with being continually humiliated by next doors fat ginger tom without adding a bird to the list too.

Concerned I'd be late picking up my fare, I got out of the car and by clapping my hands and making as much noise as I could, I eventually managed to shepherd it safely onto the pavement. Only for the cocky little git to strut back in the road as soon as I got back in my taxi and put my seatbelt back on.

Three times I got out and ushered it out of the way, but no matter how far it waddled off or how fast I rushed back to the car, as soon as I looked up it was back out on the bloody road again.

After that, I decided enough was enough. Once I'd ushered it out of the way for the fourth time, I pretended to get back in the car, slammed the door shut, and ducked down out of sight. Then as soon as it doubled back into the road, I leapt out in front of it like some kind of homicidal scarecrow and chased the surprised looking bird across the fields, whooping like an Indian and flailing my arms about until it eventually got the message and flew away over the trees.

As far as I was concerned that was the end of the matter. Honour had been restored and the human pigeon pecking order had been firmly re-established. At least I did until as I was driving around Glossop tonight, my windscreen and bonnet was suddenly splattered by a bucketful of bird shit.

Now while obviously I've got no proof it was the same bird, judging by how big the droppings were I'm pretty sure it wasn't a bloody sparrow that did it.

Sometimes diary, you just have to admit you were beaten by the better bird.

Sunday 25th May

Received a text from Carol asking if Helen and I were home tonight as she was thinking of calling round for a brew and a chat. The word 'chat' was typed in capital letters and was accompanied by an ominous looking wink.

The last thing I need is Carol turning up on my doorstep again, so I told her Helen and I were going out for the evening and we wouldn't be back until at least eleven o clock.

I wouldn't have put it past Carol deciding to call round anyway, so to be on the safe side I tried to persuade Helen and Sophie we should go out for a few hours, but because Coronation Street was about to start my wife and daughter steadfastly refused to budge.

I said, "There's more to life than sitting at home watching Steve McDonald going through another marriage crisis. Sometimes it's nice to be spontaneous at the weekend and do things off the cuff. Don't you think so?"

Helen said, "Of course, but next time you decide to do something off the cuff make sure there's nothing good on the telly first."

Thankfully, by the end of the evening there was no sign of Carol but it didn't stop me spending the night worrying and leaping off the sofa at every single sound. When the window cleaner called to collect his money as he does every fortnight, I shouted, "I'll get it," and almost knocked my wife over in my haste to get to the door first.

When I came back in, Helen said, "I know the window cleaner is a nice man but you were a bit keen to answer the door, weren't you, Eric?"

"Maybe dad was expecting a takeaway," said Sophie, without looking up from the television.

Thinking on my feet, I said, "If you must know there was a smudge on the bedroom window. I just wanted to mention it to him so he didn't miss it next time he comes."

"That's it dad," Said Sophie, "Make sure you get your three pounds a fortnight worth out of him. We don't want to see him slacking off." Then she and my wife turned to each other on the sofa and started giggling together.

It's nice to know I still have an important role to play in this family. Even if it's only as the butt of everyone else's jokes.

Monday 26th May

Dropped off a fare near home this morning so I thought I'd take the opportunity to pop back and use the bathroom. During my younger days I could have got through a whole day in the taxi without having to visit the little boy's room. Unfortunately, as I've gotten older, not only do I have to get up at least twice a night, but when I'm driving the cab I can barely look at my flask of coffee without feeling the urgent need to strain the potatoes.

I parked up outside the house, rushed inside, ran upstairs and flung open the bathroom door. Only to find Andrew laying in the bath with his equally naked girlfriend Abigail, lying opposite, vigorously washing him with a soapy sponge.
I'm still not sure who was the most surprised. Although judging by the high pitched screams, and how fast they both leapt to their feet, causing a wave of water to cascade all over the bathroom floor, I'm guessing it was probably them.

"Jesus Christ dad," screamed Andrew, reaching for the towel, while Abigail tried unsuccessfully to hide behind the flannel, "What the hell do you think you're doing?"

"Well, there's no need to ask you the same question," I said, covering my eyes with my hands. "It's fairly bloody obvious what you two are up to."

"We didn't think anyone would be home."

"I should hope you didn't. I'd hate to think you'd be getting up to this sort of thing if you thought your mother and I were downstairs watching Loose Women."

After using the bathroom for a slightly more mundane purpose than it had previously been used for, and a rather sheepish looking Abigail had left for home, I took my son to one side and advised him on the importance of locking the door when having a bath. And more importantly, not using my house as some kind of illicit sex den.

It was bad enough knowing he was getting more than me in the shed, without adding the bathroom to the list of places I was being orgasmically top trumped by my son.

Tuesday 27th May

I've just realised that even though little Eric was momentarily in the presence of a naked nineteen year old woman yesterday, he hardly even noticed. While it's true I may have been slightly distracted by being desperate for a wee, there was a time even that wouldn't have stopped him popping up for a better look. This really isn't good, diary. This really isn't good at all.

Wednesday 28th May

Another quiet day at work. Apart from a brief excursion to Tesco to buy some new bathroom sponges, I seemed to spend most of it sitting on the taxi rank waiting for non-existent customers to turn up.

The summer is never a good time for a taxi driver. As the weathers a bit warmer, people suddenly take it upon themselves to start walking everywhere. All well and good as far as their health is concerned, but it doesn't do anything to put food on my table.

Even working the late shift isn't as busy as it is during the winter months. Because it doesn't go dark until late, people who normally take a taxi because they don't feel safe walking home, are now confidently strolling about in the evening sunshine without a care in the world.

I was in Duke's cafe earlier with Harry and Paul, two of the other drivers, and I suggested if business got any slower we should spread a rumour around Glossop that there'd been a couple of murders in the area, to try and drive people back to the cabs.

I was only joking but Harry and Paul's faces lit up like a couple of Christmas trees. "You know, that's not a bad idea Eric," said Harry, scratching his chin. "How would you go about doing something like that?"

I said, "Oh, for pity's sake Harry, I wasn't being serious. We can't go around making up stories about people being murdered. Apart from it being morally wrong, I'm pretty sure it's against the law."

"Well, alright," said Paul. "Not a murder, but what about a mugging? I can't see anything wrong with that. There's bound to be someone being whacked over the head and having their purse stolen somewhere in Glossop, so it's probably true anyway.

I was about to tell him to stop being so ridiculous, when one of the women from the next table spun round in her seat. "Excuse me," She said, looking rather concerned. "Is that right what you've been saying? There's been a mugging in the area?"

"We think so," Said Harry, interrupting me before I had a chance to squash the rumour, "At least, that's what we've all heard anyway." Then he and Harry vigorously nodded at each other.

"Oh my gosh, that's awful," said the woman, looking back at her friend. "You're not safe anywhere these days, are you?"

When I drove away a few minutes later, a grinning Harry and Paul were helping the two women into their taxis. Making up muggings might not be very ethical, but it's clearly a lot more lucrative than sitting on the taxi rank for hours on end.

Thursday 29th May

I've just logged on Facebook and there's already a warning on the local group page about a spate of muggings in the area. According to rumours, there's been at least half a dozen in the last few days alone. One man even posted up a photo of his black eye, claiming it had happened last night when he was robbed outside the train station, by a gang of unruly teenagers. Not only that, but a page had been started called the Glossop vigilante group so people could volunteer their time to help keep the streets safe. They've even set up a crowdfunding page so they can afford to get their own T shirts printed.

Somehow it didn't seem right having thousands of locals worrying about being beaten up and robbed, especially when it was partly my fault they were panicking in the first place. But when I made a comment asking why we hadn't heard anything from the police or the local newspapers about these so called incidents, I was accused of being an internet troll. Me? An internet troll?

Sometimes diary, I just can't do right for doing wrong.

By the time I went to bed another three people had apparently been mugged, and one woman was claiming she'd been molested by an alien. If this imaginary crime spree gets much worse the council will probably have to think about bringing in martial law.

Friday 30th May

I've just had a really nasty experience outside the Bakers. I normally try to avoid looking at my reflection unless it's absolutely necessary, but unfortunately I was walking down the high street just as the sun disappeared behind a nearby cloud.

It was my own fault really. If I hadn't pressed my face against the glass to admire a tray of rather delicious looking fruit scones I wouldn't have suddenly come face to face with the middle aged monstrosity staring back at me in the darkened glass.

Diary, what happened to the tall, lithe, athletic, and supple skinned boy I used to know, when I was growing up?

When I was young I had such hopes and dreams, and I'm pretty sure none of those dreams involved turning into a pink wrinkle faced walrus, wearing trousers with an elastic waist.

As I stood staring back at that deadpan double chinned expression, I suddenly realised that not only had the years caught up, they'd overtaken me and were speeding down the road like a relentless juggernaut. Middle age hadn't just crept up; it had leapt out of the wardrobe and scared me half to death.

Throw in my erection issues and my non-existent sex life, and I'm beginning to wonder why I bother to get out of bed in the morning.

I was feeling so fed up it almost put me off going inside the bakers and buying three of the scones.

Diary, although they were absolutely delicious they didn't make me feel better for long. Especially as when I walked back to the car, the sun moved behind me and I realised my shadow was almost exactly the same shape as Alfred Hitchcock.

Saturday 31st May

Too depressed to write much today.

As I haven't weighed myself in a while I thought I'd climb on the scales to see if I've put on a few ounces. After stripping down to my socks and underpants I was horrified to discover when the numbers eventually stopped spinning, I now weigh 269lbs? That's eight pounds more than when I last weighed myself. According to Google, I've moved past the baby hippo stage and now weigh almost exactly the same as a teenage Walrus.

How on Earth is this possible? A couple of pounds maybe, but apart from the scones, half a dozen Pizzas', a couple of chocolate bars, the occasional fish and chips, and a bottle of wine now and again, I've barely eaten over the last few weeks, never mind put on eight bloody pounds.

I was convinced the scales must have been faulty, but when I mentioned it to Helen and Sophie they both decided to weigh themselves to prove I was wrong. Sophie was so concerned she stepped on and off the scales at least half a dozen times to prove they were working properly.

"You see, dad," She said, grinning from ear to ear as she repeatedly jumped on and off. "They seem to be working perfectly fine for me and mum."

I sometimes wonder whether my daughter actually wants me to fail at life.

Helen, on the other hand, wasn't saying much at all. When I asked her why she wasn't having a go at me for putting on weight again, she just shrugged her shoulders, and said, "What's the point, Eric? You never listen to me anyway."

It's not going to be easy, but I really need to start being more disciplined with this diet. Helen being cross with me is one thing, but the look of disappointment in her eyes as she trudged back down the stairs is one I never want to experience again.

Sunday 1st June

Things were a lot busier at work tonight. Because of the rumour going round about the amount of violent crime in the area my takings have practically doubled over the last few days. Almost every fare I picked up was asking me if I'd heard anything about all the recent muggings, or were claiming to be the victim of a crime themselves.

One rather excited gentleman even told me how he'd called in the cab office for a taxi last week and saw a rather large woman indecently exposing herself, while leaning back in a leather chair.

Honestly diary, you'd have thought Carol would have had the good sense to lock the office door first.

Monday 2nd June

I'm so hungry. I've only been back on the diet for a few days, but it already feels like it's been going on forever. When I was at work earlier, I picked up a couple of teenage lads from the centre of Glossop and dropped them off at the kebab shop.

I'm still not sure how I managed to stop myself from following them inside when I caught sight of that delicious brown meaty thing spinning away in the corner. Especially when I saw the sign in the window advertising a portion of half price chips with every kebab.

Trust me to go on a diet when they're selling half price chips. The way my luck has been going lately I'll probably find out Gregg's are having a clearance sale on sausage rolls and steak bakes.

Tuesday 3rd June

I still can’t stop thinking about food. All I’ve had to eat today is a small bowl of cornflakes, an apple and banana for lunch, and kippers on toast for tea.

I don’t even like bloody kippers. I only had them because I read online that omega three Can help thin the blood, and has occasionally been known to help with erection problems.

Not that they did anything to help me. I didn’t even feel a twinge while I was eating them, never mind anything else.

I thought Helen would have been pleased when she saw I was making more of an effort with my diet but all she could say was, “I’ve seen it all before, Eric. You’ll stick to your guns for a couple of days, but before you know it you’ll be loosening the elastic on your pants again.”

I really am determined to prove her wrong this time. Hopefully the next time I’m loosening the elastic on my pants, it’ll be to release a rampaging little Eric rather than anything else.

Wednesday 4th June

Called into Duke’s cafe earlier hoping to sit down for a few minutes and enjoy a quiet cup of coffee and a bowl of soup, while staring longingly at their delicious looking cakes.

When I arrived, Harry, Paul, and to my complete and utter dismay, Carol, were already there, chatting away in the corner.
It seems even the sanctuary of my favourite coffee shop isn't safe from that woman's wanton clutches these bloody days.
I was about to turn around and walk straight back out, but before I had a chance Carol spotted me and raced across the room.

"Eric," she screeched, linking my arm and guiding me reluctantly back to their table. "What a nice surprise. I didn't think you'd be here?"

I sighed, "You knew I was coming in today, didn't you?"

Carol looked up at me and grinned. "Well, Harry may have mentioned that you like to pop in of a lunchtime. But don't worry. I promise not to do anything to embarrass you in front of your friends."

The next twenty minutes were sheer torture. Not only was I trying to eat my lunch while fending off Carol's wandering hands underneath the table, causing the majority of the soup I was trying to eat to spill down my shirt. I also had to endure Harry and Paul bragging about how much more their takings had shot up recently. The fact it was all down to a rumour I had accidentally started, didn’t seem to bother either of them in the slightest. If anything, they seemed to be revelling in it.

“I made over a hundred pounds yesterday,” boasted Harry, sounding more like a proud father than the purveyor of gossip we both knew he was. “Even for a Tuesday that’s pretty good going. Wouldn't you say so, Eric?”

“I took even more than that,” said Paul, grinning at me from behind his coffee cup. “I’m making so much money I might even take tonight off. What do you think about that Eric?”

“Who said crime doesn’t pay?” Said Harry.

Paul chuckled. “Well, whoever he was, he certainly wasn’t a taxi driver.”

I honestly couldn’t believe the nerve of the pair. Harry was even talking about putting an advert in the local newspaper offering a discount to former mugging victims.

After listening to Carol telling us that the office had been so busy recently they were thinking of taking on extra drivers, while simultaneously trying to slap her hand away from my thigh, I decided I’d had more than enough for one day, and got up to leave.

Carol said, “You leaving already, Eric? Good, you can give me a lift home.” Then before I had a chance to refuse, she stood up and began gathering together her belongings.

Talk about presumptuous. The last thing I wanted to do was go anywhere near Carol's flat. Never mind having to fight her off in the car again.

Fortunately, as I stood trying to think of an excuse, Harry, who, despite being in his early sixties, had always had a bit of a crush on Carol, unwittingly came to my rescue and offered to give her a ride home himself.

Carol wasn't very keen but as Harry doesn't live too far from her it was difficult for her to say no. Especially as Harry was still milking the fictional crime spree for all it was worth.

"It saves Eric going out of his way," He said, "And we can't have you wandering the streets alone now, can we Carol? It isn't safe out there you know. Not with all this violent crime in the area."

Carol shook her head, "Oh, you don't have to worry about me. I'm more than capable of looking after myself." Then she suddenly grabbed a surprised looking Harry by the arm, twisted it around his back, and pushed him hard up against the wall. Almost knocking a couple of unsuspecting customers over in the process. "See?"

Harry, who was clearly struggling to breathe with Carol's breasts pressed against his back nodded enthusiastically. "I didn't doubt it for a second," He croaked.

I didn't doubt it for a second either. If it came down to a straight fight between Carol and a make believe criminal I'd put my money on the latter going home penniless and probably without his trousers every single time.

2.15pm

Received a text from Carol telling me the journey home would have been a lot more fun if I'd been the one driving her, and was accompanied by a photo of her kissing the camera lens.
I think it was designed to turn me on but all the picture did was remind me I'd forgotten to Sky plus the Les Dawson special on UK gold. Even if little Eric had been working properly I doubt that picture would have been enough to grab his attention. Especially as she'd forgotten to pluck her nostril hair before taking the photo.

2.48pm

Received a text from Harry, that simply said, 'What a woman!'
I didn't reply. If only he knew the bloody half of it

Thursday 5th June

As we were sitting down to eat tonight (a very small bowl of chicken casserole and no dumpling for me) the door suddenly flew open and Andrew came rushing in, red faced, and hopping about from one foot to the other. “You’ll never guess what’s happened?” he said.

It was obviously big news because Sophie stopped eating and put down her spoon. Something that was unheard of unless there was an urgent text asking her ‘what she was up to?’ that needed replying to. “You don’t mean…?” she asked, looking up at him expectantly.

Andrew nodded and beamed from ear to ear. Encouraging Sophie to abandon her normal air of aloofness, leap up from her chair, and throw her arms around him.

To see Andrew smiling was unusual enough by itself. For him and Sophie to hug it out was an event even rarer than a solar eclipse.

“That’s brilliant,” she said. “You’re going to be amazing, I just know it.”

Helen and I meanwhile just looked at each other gormlessly. “So are you going to tell us what’s going on,” said Helen, “or shall we just read about it on Facebook later when you update your statuses?”

I said, “Maybe he’s got himself a job interview.”

Andrew rolled his eyes. “Don’t be ridiculous dad. I’d have to actually apply for a job to get one of those. No, this is much better than that,” he said, grinning broadly again. “I’ve only gone and got myself a gig.”

When we asked how this had all come about, Andrew told us how Abigail the emo and animal rights activist had recently started work at The Wheatsheaf (a local pub and occasional live music venue) and had put his name forward when she found out they were on the lookout for new talent. Then, after going down and singing a few songs, they inexplicably invited our son to perform live to the actual public. There really is no accounting for taste.

Helen said, “I thought Abigail was working at McDonalds?”

Andrew nodded. “She was, but you know what these fast food places are like mum. Seems they didn’t like Abby reminding the diners how many cows and pigs had been sacrificed so they could stuff their faces with burgers, sausages, and chicken nuggets. Then just because on her day off she stood outside handing out ‘Meat is Murder’ leaflets to people as they were going in, they go and give her the sack. They didn’t even give her a warning or anything.”

“Some people,” I said, shaking my head in bewilderment. “Has she thought about suing them for unfair dismissal?”

“You know this is so cool,” said Sophie, completely ignoring me. “I can’t believe you’re going to be singing on a proper stage at a proper venue. You’re going to be, like famous, and everything.”

“Whoa, slow down,” said Andrew. “Let’s not get too carried away. I’m only going to be singing a few songs at

The Wheatsheaf. It's not like I'm going on Britain's Got Talent."

"Yeah well, everyone famous had to start somewhere," Said Sophie, who obviously had a lot more faith in her brother than I did. "I'm going to tell Mel and Tim."

As Sophie strode purposefully into the lounge texting away ten to the dozen as she went, Andrew turned to us and asked, "So, are you and mum going to come and watch me then?"

"I suppose so," I said. "Just as long as there's nothing good on the telly."

Helen slapped me playfully on the wrist. "Your Father's joking. We're all going to come and support you. Were both really proud of you, aren't we, Eric?"

I nodded. "Of course we are. Goes without saying."

Telling Andrew I was proud of him wasn't something I had the chance to tell him very often these days. Mostly because it just wouldn't have been true. It's difficult to be proud of a workshy teenager who spends his days living in a shed, watching hard-core pornography, and having rampant, uncomplicated sex with your next door neighbour's daughter. Even if it is a lifestyle I would have killed for when I was his age.

If it had been anybody else's son but mine, I probably would have given him a pat on the back but it's always different when it's your own. Other parents were able to boast about their children going off to university or climbing the career ladder, but when people ask about Andrew, I usually tell them he's planning to do some voluntary work abroad, and had moved into the garden shed so he could get used to the lifestyle of living in a ramshackle shack.

Helen thinks I'm being ridiculous, but it's partly her fault he's still in there. I doubt he'd be so keen on living in the garden if his mother wasn't hanging a pair of freshly laundered underpants to the handle of the shed door every morning.

Since Andrew moved into the shed opportunities for us to sit down together as a family are few and far between, so Helen fetched our son a plate and insisted he eat with us. Then a few minutes later Abigail the emo arrived and joined us for a bite to eat too.

As this was the first time I'd seen Abigail since finding her and my son naked together in the bathroom, things were a little awkward to begin with. But when Helen fetched her some tea and I helpfully pointed out that offering an animal rights activist a bowl of chicken casserole probably wasn't the best idea in the world, we soon got back to our old selves again.

I have to say that despite how hungry I was feeling watching them all eat; it was still rather nice listening to lots of chatter and laughter as the kids shovelled down their food.
When it's just the three of us, the only noises you can normally hear are the television in the background, the

message alert on Sophie's phone, and the sound of my stomach grumbling.

Friday 6th June

Can you believe it? Next door's cat has been in my kitchen again. That animal is spending so much time in my house these days I may as well install a bloody cat flap.

It must have snuck inside when I took the rubbish out earlier, and when I went to make a cup of tea, there it was, bold as brass, standing on the counter scratching on the microwave door. That's the last time I cook kippers in this house. The smell lingers for days.

Honestly diary, I couldn't believe the nerve of the thing. When it saw me it didn't even flinch. It just dismissed me like I was non entity, started licking its lips, and then turned its attention back to the bloody microwave again.

That was enough for me. After opening the back door, I grabbed a couple of pans and began chasing it around the kitchen, banging them together as loudly as possible as I tried to frighten it off. I must have been chasing it for a good two minutes before it eventually got the message and scarpered back out into the garden.

Helen and Sophie had come running in from the lounge to see what all the commotion was. Only to find me bent over double holding a saucepan in one hand and a frying pan in the other as I struggled for breath.

When I told them what'd happened Helen said, "Bloody hell, Eric. You can't just go around hitting cats with pots and pans you know. This is real life, not an episode of Tom & Jerry."

While Sophie added, "It's just a cat dad. What did it ever do to you?"

I tried explaining that all I was trying to do was get it out of the kitchen, but I'm not entirely convinced they believed me. Then to make matters worse, Andrew and Abigail came in from the garden with next door's cat wrapped up in a swaddling blanket like some sort of fat ginger baby. "What's going on?" said Andrew. "We just found him cowering behind the shed?"

"He's frightened to death," said Abigail stroking his brow with her finger.

As I looked on Helen and Sophie rushed over to help. "Oh, the poor little thing," Said Helen. "Quick, fetch it inside where it's nice and warm."

Diary, I really didn't know what was going on. One minute I was chasing the cat out of the kitchen and the next it was back inside being stroked by my wife, Sophie, Andrew and Abigail, as it was sitting on my kitchen counter, drinking a saucer of my bloody milk. Talk about taking the bloody piss.

Later, I logged onto Facebook and sent my neighbour the following message:

Dear Ron,

I just thought I would let you know that earlier today I found your fat ginger tom foraging for food in my kitchen. While I appreciate it's always going to be difficult to stop your cat from wandering into my garden, a man's home is his castle, and if I find that beast of yours has crossed the boundaries of the kitchen door portcullis just one more time I'm afraid I will be not be responsible for my actions.

Your neighbour and friend, Eric.

Five minutes later I received the following response.

Dear Eric,

I can only once again apologise while at the same time marvelling at the coincidence. Earlier today, I returned home from work and found your son foraging for food in MY kitchen. Indeed, at one point his head was so far inside the fridge he was in danger of catching frostbite.
It would seem, Eric, I'm not the only one with a large hairy mammal that likes to raid next doors castle for a snack.

Your neighbour and friend, Ron.

Saturday 7th June

Woke up in a cold sweat last night after experiencing an erotic nightmare about Helen. In my dream I was sitting watching television while Helen was on the exercise bike. I was trying to concentrate on what Steve and Liz McDonald were arguing about in the back of the rovers, but out of the corner of my eye I could see Helen eying me up and down, undressing me with her ravenous eyes, and slowly licking her lips. Eventually I couldn't take it anymore, so I pressed mute on the remote and turned towards her.

"Will you stop looking at me like that," I said. "I'm a human being, not a piece of bloody meat. Just get on with your workout woman."

Helen smiled, climbed off the bike and began advancing catlike towards me. "Oh, shut up Eric," She said, wiping the sweat from her brow with the back of her hand. "Why don't you go upstairs and run us both a bath. I'll be up in a minute."

Diary, I don't think I've ever run so fast in my life. I was just beginning to pour in the bubble bath when Helen came up behind me and began running her finger delicately up my spine. I turned towards her as she took a step backwards, her eyes never leaving mine as she began removing her clothes. Once completely naked Helen then kissed me lingeringly on the lips, and stepped slowly into the water.

"Well, don't just stand there looking stupid Eric," She said, once she'd settled beneath the bubbles. "Are you getting undressed today or not?"

Even though it was only a dream I didn't need to be asked twice. I pulled off my shirt and tie, and they were quickly followed by my trousers and underpants. However, just as I was about to climb in beside her Helen suddenly shrieked out loud and jabbed repeatedly at my genitals.

"What the hell's that?" she shouted.

I quickly looked down to see what she was pointing at, but rather than seeing little Eric glaring back up at me there was nothing there whatsoever. I was like a human version of action man.

I can only assume my missing genitals are my subconscious mind's way of dealing with my erection issues. Either that, or I've just had a premonition of what will happen to them if Helen ever finds out about Carol.

In my dream I started to shriek even louder than my wife and immediately woke myself up. I sometimes wish I could wake myself up from reality too.

Sunday 8th June

Helen and I went shopping this morning. Or rather Helen went shopping while I dutifully followed behind, pushing the trolley, as she filled it up with seemingly every low fat, less tasty option she could find.

Shopping is a depressing enough experience as it is without throwing healthy food into the mix too. It didn't help that as she took them off the shelves, Helen was presenting every item to me like she was some kind of game show assistant. I tried to look enthusiastic as she held them out to me with her eyebrows raised as she sought out my approval, but it's difficult to feign excitement when you come face to face with a stick of celery or a packet of wholemeal rice crackers. However, as I'm determined not to slip off the wagon this time, that's exactly what I did. I nodded and smiled at every single item, and said, "They look nice," and watched forlornly as she dropped them in the trolley. Maybe if I say it often enough, then by the time I come to eat them I may actually believe it.

It seemed to take forever, but once finished, we headed outside and loaded up the car. I'd just started the engine, and was looking around, doing my usual safety checks, when I spotted Carol in the rear view mirror, fast approaching from behind. She was puffing and panting and waving a couple of shopping bags in the air as she tried to attract our attention.

It reminded me of the scene in Jurassic park where they're being chased by the Tyrannosaurus Rex and they can see it closing in on them in the wing mirror. The main difference being seeing Carol advancing towards you with her claws outstretched is a lot more bloody frightening.

Thankfully, I managed to speed away before she reached us otherwise Helen would have insisted we give her a lift home. Knowing Carol, I doubt there's anything she would have liked more than watching me squirm as she and Helen chatted away beside me.

Later, as I was putting away the shopping, I received a text from Carol. It said, 'I know you knew I was behind you Eric. I saw your eyes widen in the mirror.'

I replied with, 'I have no idea what you're wittering on about woman. 'My wife' and I have been shopping all morning so I haven't had a chance to see either you or anybody else.'

Carol said, 'A likely story Eric. Maybe if you hadn't done a wheel spin and almost knocked that old lady over as you were speeding out of the car park, I might have believed you.'

This time I didn't reply. Experience has taught me it's sometimes better to stop digging and throw away the shovel, before you've reached the bottom of the hole.

Monday 9th June

As Helen was working late and Sophie was having her tea at the ginger gorilla's, I thought I'd grab the opportunity to fire up the laptop and do some more research on erection issues.

Although why I bothered I really don't know. By the end, I was even more confused than when I first started. There are so many groups and web pages dedicated to the subject I'm surprised there's any room on the internet for anything else.

Hoping to find a quick fix solution I anonymously joined a couple of groups and posted up a list of my symptoms and as much background information as I could remember. I even included the segments about Carol and the Snicker's wrapper, as well as Abigail and the soapy sponge.

By the time I logged off the thread had received over three hundred replies and had been nominated for post of the month.

As far as I could tell by the responses I received, although I should really discuss it with a doctor, the consensus of opinion was in my case the cause is much more likely to be psychological rather than physical.

Or to put it another way, it's all bloody Carol's fault.

I also discovered erectile dysfunction is so common these days almost every male is likely to experience it at some point during their lives. So on the plus side, even if he hasn't already, there's a good chance my next door neighbour's fat ginger tom will suffer from it at some time in the future. I know it's not much of a consolation but it certainly made me feel a little bit better.

Tuesday 10th June

Helen and I have just had a massive argument. Or rather I stood open mouthed while my wife threw things around the kitchen and had a completely unnecessary rant about how pathetic I am.

According to Helen, I'm a fat useless waste of space, a bone idle lump of lard, a complete and utter tosspot, a dipstick, and a bald headed pillock.

It all started when I arrived home from work. I'd just done another ten hour shift in the taxi, my back was aching, my stomach was grumbling, and then I walked in the kitchen to find Helen making me a cheese and tomato salad for tea.

Honestly diary, I know I'm supposed to be on a diet but there was hardly enough cheese there to feed an anorexic titmouse, never mind a fully grown man. Although I still think Helen's reaction was slightly over the top, I certainly didn't deserve to have a tomato and handful of wet lettuce thrown at my face. If I hadn't ducked out of the way quite so quickly I might have been seriously injured.

"You're just so bloody ungrateful Eric," She said, vigorously spooning the rest of the food she hadn't thrown at me into the kitchen bin. "I try to do something nice for you and this is the thanks I get. Well from now on you're on your own, because I for one won't be lifting a finger to help in the future. Do you hear me? Not one bloody finger."

"Well, I'm sorry," I said, "But I've barely eaten anything all day. I was just hoping for something a bit more substantial than a plate of rabbit food for tea."

"I thought you were back on the diet, or is that out of the window again already?"

"No, of course it isn't." I protested. "It isn't easy but I'm sticking to it."

"Oh, are you sure?" Said Helen. "Because if you like I can always nip out and get us some fish, chips and mushy peas for tea? You'll probably have to ask me and Sophie to test the scales again for you later, but what does that matter as long as it tastes good, right?"

Diary, I really didn't mean to pause. As soon as Helen mentioned all that delicious sounding food I couldn't stop the images popping in my mind. I'd already eaten most of the chips and mushy peas, and had just made a start on the fish when Helen's voice suddenly snapped me back to reality.

"You're actually thinking about it right now, aren't you?" She said. "It's no wonder you can't stop piling on the pounds. It's all you ever think about."

"It's not my fault," I said, "You're the one who put the idea in my head."

Helen brushed past me and headed into the hall. "Well, I've had enough. You do whatever you want Eric. Eat yourself to death if you like. Just don't expect me to stick around and watch you do it." Then she put on her coat and stormed round to her parent's house.

Although I only found out that's where she went, because half an hour later I received a text from her mother calling me an ungrateful male chauvinist pig.

I did think about going after her. But I learned a long time ago, that when hurricane Helen puts in an appearance, it's always best to let it blow itself out before you emerge from the cellar. Otherwise, you're just going to get knocked off your feet again.

It was gone eleven, and I was already in bed by the time Helen came home. I had hoped a few hours with her mum and dad might have calmed her down, but if anything, it seemed to have made matters worse.

"I'll clean the tomato off the kitchen window then, shall I Eric?" She bellowed up the stairs. "No honestly, it's fine. Don't you put yourself out, you good for nothing bone idle sod."

Wednesday 11th June

Helen still isn’t talking to me. Instead of coming home after work today she went straight round to her mother’s again and didn’t return until well after nine. When arrived I greeted her at the door with a smile and a cup of tea, but Helen completely ignored me and went straight upstairs to sleep in Andrew’s room.

Just as I was beginning to think things couldn’t get any worse, I received a text from Carol saying she hopes Helen and I manage to get our marriage back on track, but if I ever need a sympathetic shoulder to cry on, I know exactly where she is. I've been avoiding replying to Carol's texts recently for fear of encouraging her, but as her message seemed a bit too close to home I felt I had no other choice. After deliberating for a few moments I replied with, 'Thank you for your kind offer but I have no idea what you’re talking about, woman. Helen and I are perfectly fine, thank you very much.’

Carol text back, 'Oh, pull the other one Eric, it’s got bells on.”

Diary, it seems after storming out of the house last night my wife rang the cab office. Her parents only live round the corner, so Helen would normally walk, but because she'd read on Facebook about all the crime in the area she decided to call for a taxi. As soon as Carol recognised Helen’s voice and how upset she was, she leapt on the opportunity and asked her if she wanted to meet up for lunch and a glass of wine. Talk about bad luck. Apparently Karma isn’t too bothered about who it pays back for their wrongdoings anymore; it just takes everything out on me instead.

Diary, during their meal, not only had my wife told her all about my recent weight gain and my lack of interest in the bedroom, she'd even told her about my dirty underpants too.

I tried to play it down by saying Helen was exaggerating because we'd just had a row, but Carol said, 'You've already told me you don't have sex anymore Eric. And after that night together at my place, I know she's not exaggerating about your underpants.'

I asked Carol what else they'd been talking about but all she'd say was 'Wouldn't you like to know?' Then stopped replying to my texts.

The only thing I can be certain of is that Carol hasn't told her anything about what almost happened between us. If she had, Helen wouldn't be sleeping in our son's room again tonight. She'd be back in the bedroom with me, battering me to death with a shovel.

Thursday 12th June

My wife is beginning to thaw a little. Instead of completely ignoring me and pretending I no longer exist, she has now decided to communicate with me via our daughter, instead.

During breakfast, Helen said, "Sophie, ask your father whether he wants one slice of toast or two?"

When I replied, 'Just one as I'm still on a diet,' Helen bounced across the table a slice of the blackest looking toast I've ever seen. My wife mumbled something about the toaster playing up, but it seemed to be working perfectly fine again a few minutes later when she produced a plateful of delicious looking golden slices for her and Sophie.

She hadn't even bothered to butter mine properly. Helen just stuck a massive dollop in the middle of the bread and then threw the knife across the table. "Tell your father he can butter his own," She said.

As we were eating, Sophie, who was obviously enjoying watching me suffer, kept glancing across at me and licking her lips, "This toast is really nice mum. In fact, it's probably one of the nicest pieces of toast I've ever eaten. Are you not eating yours, dad?"

I scowled at my daughter from behind my hand. "Yes, of course I am," I said, trying to force down another mouthful of buttered charcoal. "I'm really enjoying it if you must know."

After a brief pause, Sophie said, "So, are you and dad going to get divorced, mum?"

Helen said, "I shouldn't think so. Not as long as your father sorts himself out."

"Well, that's good," Said Sophie. "My weekends are busy enough as it is without having to visit dad in a crappy bedsit every other Sunday."

I wasn't sure my daughter was entirely joking, but it certainly raised a brief smile from Helen. At least it did until she caught me smiling back at her. After that her face suddenly reverted back to its sucking-a-lemon expression again.

Things still weren't much better by the evening. I tried to prove I was making more of an effort by climbing on the exercise bike and cycling away a few hundred calories, but Helen was being her usual stubborn self and barely even acknowledged I was in the room, no matter how loud I panted.

“Well, I feel a lot better after that,” I lied, as I climbed off the bike. Desperately trying to keep my knees from buckling by leaning against the handlebars. “It’s amazing how energetic you feel after a good workout. I can certainly see why you’re so addicted to this exercise lark, Helen. I think I’ll be fighting you for first go in the future.”

Helen said to Sophie, “Tell your father there’s no need to lay it on quite so thick. Let’s just see how long it lasts this time, shall we.”

It may not have been the enthusiasm I was hoping for, but at least it was a step in the right direction.

Friday 13th June

After last night's vigorous workout I was certain the elastic of my pyjama bottoms felt a little bit looser this morning, so I jumped on the scales and was amazed to discover I now weigh just under 266lbs. That means during the last few days of dieting I've lost nearly 4lbs. That's almost a third of a stone. I know I've barely eaten anything during the last week, particularly since falling out with Helen, but it still came as a bit of a shock. The being-in-the-doghouse diet obviously works a treat.

I was feeling so pleased, that when I got home from work I jumped on the exercise bike again and cycled away another three hundred calories.

I could tell Helen was impressed by my new found eagerness. She may not have offered much in the way of encouragement but when the pedals started squeaking during a particularly tense scene in *Neighbours,* she didn't even bother to tell me to shut up once.

Saturday 14th June

All I've had to eat today is two rounds of toast, a bowl of instant porridge and a banana for lunch, fish, boiled potatoes and green beans for tea, and an apple for supper. If things carry on like this I'll be back to my ideal weight in next to no time.

Sunday 15th June

Father's day today. An entire year since Helen and I last made love. Going by how things are between Helen and myself, I'd say the chances of an anniversary re-enactment are pretty much non-existent. Although given little Eric's predicament, that's probably a good thing.

Only received two cards this year. No presents. That's an even worse return than I had on my birthday.

Sophie's card read:

Happy Father's day dad.
Hope you liked the socks.
Lots of love
Sophie.

I asked, what socks, and Sophie said, "It's those ones I gave you on your birthday? They were a joint present for Father's day too."

When she saw the look on my face she added, "Well, I keep telling you I should be on more pocket money. It's an expensive job being a teenage girl."

Mind you, at least my daughter bothered to write the card herself. At first I didn't even recognise the handwriting in the one from Andrew. It certainly wasn't his or his mother's. It was only when I noticed the card had been addressed to Mr Baxter, rather than dad, I realised it had been written by Abigail.

Happy Father's day, me.

In an attempt to get back in her good books I offered to take Helen, Sophie and Andrew out for a Father's day meal. I even told Helen to invite her parents along too.

When it comes to food John and Mary tend to eat like a couple of hungry hippos so I knew it wouldn't be easy watching them fill their faces, but better that than getting the nearly silent treatment every night.

Being practically ignored may have guaranteed my wife wouldn't be searching out my genitals any time soon, but I hate it when there's an atmosphere in the house. Even Sophie seemed to be getting less pleasure out of it, and she normally revels in watching me suffer.

When I went outside to invite Andrew I could hear loud music coming from the shed. At first I thought he was practising for his gig next week but when I saw the shed door rattling so fast it was almost coming off its hinges, I guessed he and Abigail were probably otherwise engaged.

Where those two get their energy from, I've no idea. They're at it in the garden more often that next door's bloody cat.

Not that they were the only ones. When we arrived at Helen's parents it took them a good five minutes to answer the door. When it did eventually open a rather flustered looking Mary was straightening her glasses, buttoning up her blouse, and had her skirt on the wrong way round.

At first we thought they were just running behind, but when we followed Mary into the lounge we found an equally red-faced John hurriedly tucking his shirt into his pants.

“Is it that time already?” He said, winking at Mary who was busying herself plumping the buttock shaped sofa cushions. “We haven’t had a chance to work up a proper Father’s day appetite yet, have we love?”

I couldn’t believe it. It seems even Helen’s parents have a better sex life than me, and John has more health issues than a Christmas episode of *Holby City*.

Helen and Sophie meanwhile, looked absolutely horrified. Helen’s eyes were wider than a couple of dinner plates as she stood clutching her dad’s card and present, and Sophie’s face was wearing an expression of terror I hadn’t seen since she found out we’d thrown away all the chocolate biscuits.

“Oh my God! Please, just shoot me right now,” She said. “This is officially the most embarrassing moment of my life, ever! And I live with dad. Please mum, tell me they're not my real grandparents and you were actually adopted?”

Helen said, “I only wish I was. What in Earth were you two thinking of?”

“I think it’s fairly obvious what they were thinking of,” Said Sophie, screwing up her face.

John said, “We were only doing what nature intended. If we hadn’t done it in the first place then neither you nor our granddaughter would be here to kick up a fuss about it now.” Then he reached down to the floor to pick up his belt. Unfortunately a natural consequence of reaching for his belt was he let go of his trousers and they instantly dropped down to his ankles.

I don’t know why, but I’d always thought of my father in law as an underpants kind of man. To find out he was wearing a tiny black thong came as something of a revelation.

“Right, that’s it,” Shrieked Sophie, staring aghast at her grandfather’s buttocks. “If anybody wants me, I’ll be in the car phoning ChildLine.”

“Text me the number,” Said Helen. “I think I'll be phoning too.”

I said, “Well, you better not ring at the same time otherwise you’ll both be engaged.”

That probably wasn’t the best moment to try and lighten the atmosphere. Judging by the snarls I received from Helen and Sophie, I’m guessing they thought the same.

Despite the awkward start, the rest of the day seemed to go rather well. For lunch I had lamb, two roast potatoes, and as much mixed veg as I could pile on my plate.

When the pudding was served John and Mary kept trying to tempt me to try some of theirs, but I was determined not to overindulge, and filled up my plate with even more vegetables instead.

“A few drops of custard won’t do you any harm,” Said Mary, waving her spoon at me from across the table. “You can put it on a bit of my rhubarb crumble if you like. You’ll hardly even feel it going down.”

“Go on,” Said John, “You know what they say. A little bit of what you fancy does you good. Isn’t that right Mary love.” Then he reached across and slapped her playfully on the thigh.

Sophie wasn't saying very much during the meal, but that was mostly because she was busy telling Melody, the ginger gorilla, and everybody else on Facebook and twitter, how traumatised she was. She’d even posted up a picture of a tiny black thong along with the status:

That moment when you almost catch your grandparents doing it and you find out your grandad wears a pair of these

#embarrassinggrandparents
#someonepleaseadoptme
#oneofhistesticleswashangingoutabit

When Helen asked her to delete it and not wash our family's dirty laundry in public, John told her to leave it up as he quite enjoyed being an internet star. He even asked Sophie to create him and Mary an account so they could tag themselves in.

By the time we arrived home Helen was beginning to communicate with me again, Sophie's status had amassed over a hundred likes, and John and Mary had joined Facebook.

Monday 16th June

Received a text from Carol telling me not to forget to put on a clean pair of underpants before bed tonight, just in case I got lucky with Helen.

She was being sarcastic, but just in case Helen decided to initiate some post Father's day, make up sex, I took off the clean pair I'd put on after my shower, fished my dirty pair out of the laundry basket, and put them back on again.
Given that Helen had only just started talking to me again, the chances of her trying to seduce me were probably less than winning the lottery, but better to be safe than sorry.

Tuesday 17th June

When I got home, I noticed we'd run out of teabags. The shops are only a couple of hundred yards from my house so normally I'd drive, but as it was a sunny day I thought the walk would do me good. Unfortunately, as I was coming out of my house Ron came out of his house at exactly the same time.

Even though we've lived next to each other for over twenty years, I've always found Ron to be a difficult person to get along with on the whole. He was a very monosyllabic character at the best of times, but since I started complaining about his cat using my garden as an outdoor litter tray all I get out of him these days is the occasional grunt.

Which is why, rather than complaining in person, I started doing it via the medium of email instead. Helen thinks I'm being cowardly and ever so slightly pathetic, but since we started talking through Facebook Ron and I have actually spoken to each other a lot more than we ever did in real life.

When I saw Ron I did think about saying hello, but there's always the danger that he might actually start talking to me again. So instead, I greeted him with obligatory polite head nod and off we went down the path towards the shops.

I was hoping Ron would turn off at some point, but after fifty yards or so it became apparent we were both walking in the same direction. I started to feel a little uncomfortable having Ron walking right next to me, not saying a word, so I picked up the pace a little and quickly moved five yards ahead of him. Next thing I could hear Ron's footsteps quicken and he'd started to gain on me again.

Rather than just let him pass like any sensible person would, I then started walking even faster. Until I was really moving rather briskly, swinging my arms from side to side like the Olympic walkers do in an attempt to stay ahead. In turn, Ron started to speed up too, and before I knew it, he was practically walking beside me again.

It was at this point I began to realise Ron and I were in a race, and just ahead of us I could see the steps and the wheelchair ramp that leads down to the shops. There was only enough room for one of us on that ramp, and I was determined that whatever happened it was going to be me.

As we approached the ramp I was beginning to flag a little. I'd lost momentum, my legs were beginning to ache, and I could feel my sweat covered shirt clinging to my body as the warm afternoon sunshine began to take its toll. As luck would have it though, Ron is equally as portly as me, and when I looked across I could see he was beginning to struggle just as much as I was.

Talk about unfit. We'd only walked about one hundred and fifty metres and he already looked as though he was about to keel over from a heart attack. That man really needs to sort himself out. He was still only just behind me however, so in an effort to stay ahead, I started using an obstruction technique. Flapping my arms about like a chicken, and varying my walking style, as I zig-zagged across the pavement trying to put him off.

It must have worked because when I looked back, I could see Ron stumbling and slowing down, until he eventually came to a stop, standing with his hands on his knees, gasping for breath in the middle of the path.

The poor man had obviously realised he was beaten, as I pumped my fist in the air and sauntered casually towards the shop. Something that wasn't easy to do considering my chest felt like it was about to explode. I was so exhausted that when I eventually staggered to the bottom of the ramp and out of sight of Ron, I had a sit down on the pavement for five minutes to try and get my breath back.
Next time we run out of teabags I think I'll just take the car.

7.48pm

Just received a Facebook message from Ron. The message read:

Dear Eric.

Just wanted to let you know that as I was looking over the garden fence earlier, I noticed my cat, Hercules, loitering around your flowerbeds while acting in a very suspicious manner.

I knew he was up to no good but before I had a chance to stop him, I saw him crouch down and take a rather large looking shit in the vicinity of your rhododendrons.

For this I can only apologise. Especially as Hercules has been suffering from a fairly severe case of diarrhoea for the last few days making his faeces practically impossible to scoop up with a shovel.

Although I do have an old sponge you can borrow if you decide to give it a go?

Your neighbour and friend, Ron.

I didn't reply. Sometimes diary, it's the small victories in life that make things worth getting out of bed for in the morning.

Wednesday 18th June

All that power walking yesterday must have done me good. I weighed myself this morning I was amazed to discover I've dropped two pounds. I've lost so much weight that when I stood on my tiptoes and craned my neck completely forward I could almost see my genitals again. Not that there's much going on down there to see at the moment.

Helen and Sophie were eating breakfast when I rushed downstairs to tell them my good news. After recent events I really wasn't expecting much support, especially from my wife. But when I told them about Ron and the walking race, and Sophie shook her head, and accused me of being Britain's most embarrassing dad again, Helen actually came to my defence.

She scowled at our daughter and told her to stop being so horrible, and that it wouldn't do her any harm to try and give me a bit of encouragement now and again.

Sophie and I just looked at each other trying to figure out which one of us was the most surprised by my wife's unexpected show of solidarity.

"I was only joking mum" Said Sophie.

Helen reached over and passed me a small bowl of porridge. "Yes, well, even I can see your fathers making more of an effort this time," She said. "Maybe walking is your thing, Eric. We've all got one exercise that seems to work better for us than anything else. I've got the exercise bike and maybe walking is yours? You can certainly tell you're losing a few pounds."

Diary, it seems like all my grovelling has finally paid off. Instead of throwing knives at me across the dining room table, my wife is actually throwing the occasional compliment. I had no idea where this change of heart came from, but I've never been one to look a gift horse in the mouth. Even if I was slightly concerned that one wrong word and that same horse would clamp its jaws around my throat and rip my bloody head off.

As Sophie was leaving for school she grabbed her satchel and paused momentarily, before turning towards me. "You know I think you've been doing really well just lately dad" She said, nodding sagely. "In fact you don't look anywhere near as fat as you did a couple of weeks ago." Then she smiled and walked out of the room.

Even now I can't decide whether she was being sarcastic or was trying to be genuinely complimentary. For the sake of my own sanity, I've decided to opt for the latter.

Thursday 19th June

All I've eaten today are a couple of shredded wheat, a salad for lunch, and a small shepherd's pie for tea. I didn't even have any supper. If I can carry on in this vein, then pretty soon I won't even need to crane my neck forward to see my genitals, I'll probably only need to look down.

Who knows, hopefully by then, little Eric will be able to look back up at me too.

Friday 20th June

Helen suggested we go for a brisk walk round the estate after work. It was my own fault really. She was going to go on her own, but because of my new found enthusiasm for exercise, and the gangs of criminals supposedly rampaging through the streets, she decided to invite me along too.

After another busy day driving, the last thing I was in the mood for was an evening of exercise, but as Helen had only just started talking to me again I didn't really feel like I was in any position to say no.

Although on the plus side part of me was thinking, as I pulled on my jogging bottoms, if Helen decided to try and sleep with me again during the next week or so at least I'd have a readymade excuse to turn her down. Telling her I'm too exhausted is a lot more preferable than telling her I haven't had a proper erection for almost a month.

Diary, judging by how fast she was moving, Helen and I clearly have different definitions of the word brisk. I thought I was travelling at a fair old lick when I defeated Ron in the race to the shops but Helen was speeding up the road even faster than Roadrunner. Every time she turned round trying to encourage me to pick up the pace, I half expected her to shout 'Beep Beep' never mind, 'Get a move on Eric. The soaps will be starting soon.'

I was also beginning to realise how embarrassed and self-conscious Carol must have felt when she pursued me down the road wearing nothing but her knickers. Normally when I exercise, it's in the privacy of my own home, where the only abuse I'm likely to receive is from Sophie. To be on the receiving end of spontaneous mockery from strangers came as something of a shock. Men were laughing, women were pointing, and a couple of children ran out of their garden shouting, "Look mummy, it's a Teletubby."

I puffed and panted up the road trying to distract myself from my misery by focussing on Helen, as she fast disappeared into the distance. Just ahead I could see a bus shelter surrounded by a fog of cigarette smoke. I was hoping I could waddle past before the occupants spotted me, but as I tried to pick up a bit of pace by pumping my arms back and forth a gang of surly looking teenage girls emerged menacingly from the nicotine mist.

The tallest girl, who was obviously the ringleader, stepped forward and looked me up and down. “Look girls,” She said, as she took a huge puff on her cigarette. “It’s Mo Farah’s dad.” Laughter.

“No, it’s not,” Said another. “It’s Usain Bolt’s mum.”

Another girl stepped forward and began jabbing repeatedly in my direction. “Hey, I know who you are. You’re that fat man who fell tit first in the wheelie bin. You remember Rach, from Facebook?”

“The tall girl grinned from ear to ear. “Oh yeah, it is. Hey mister, can we have your autograph?” You can get your arse to sign it if you like.” Yet more laughter.

As I barely had enough energy to breathe, never mind tell her to sod off, I decided to ignore them and concentrate on moving forward. But when I glanced back the girls were right behind me.

Diary, as the girls followed me not only were they taunting me and calling me names, but whenever I paused to catch my breath, they were taking it in turns to run up behind me and kick me up the arse. If that wasn't bad enough, as we were going along more and more children were coming out to join them. It was like a scene from a Rocky film. Except when Rocky Balboa was pounding the streets the kids were joining him as a show of support, not to throw sticks at him, or yell, "Get a move on granddad."

I was hoping Helen would come back to rescue me, but there was no sign of her anywhere.

Then a miracle happened. Just as I was beginning to think the children were going to abuse me all the way home, I saw what looked like a posse rounding the corner just ahead of us. There were a dozen middle-aged women, and a little old man carrying a sausage dog. They were all wearing T shirts with the words 'Glossop vigilante group' emblazoned across their chests.

The world seemed to stop for a moment as the two factions stared at each other across the street. Then a curly haired woman with Deirdre Barlow glasses stepped forward, and sounded the battle cry. "Come on you lot, let's get them." And then they were charging towards us.

As most of the participants were children and middle-aged women, I wouldn't call it a fight as such. Even the word scuffle would be slightly overdoing it. There was lots of shouting, swearing, and plenty of handbag swinging, but probably the most dangerous thing that happened was when the old man roared too loudly as he and the sausage dog chased a laughing toddler along the path and his false teeth fell out.

By the time my wife bothered to come back to see why I was taking so long, it was all over. The children had bolted down the side streets and I was being comforted by the Deirdre Barlow lookalike.

I said, “Well thanks for leaving me to it, Helen. I could have been mocked to death for all you know.”

Helen shook her head. “Stop being so melodramatic, Eric. It just sounds like a bunch of kids playing silly buggers to me.”

“Never underestimate children.” Said my rescuer. “Your husband’s a very lucky man. The teenage girls on this estate are practically feral.”

Helen said, “You don’t have to tell me. I’ve given birth to one.”

Even though it was embarrassing being rescued by middle-aged women, and an old aged pensioner and his sausage dog, I gave each of them a grateful handshake and thanked them for their help. It may have been the rumour I started that was responsible for the vigilantes being there in the first place, but right then I was bloody glad they were.

Saturday 21st June

Woken up by my mobile phone this morning. It was a Facebook notification. When I logged on Ron had shared a video to my timeline and commented 'Looks like you're really getting the hang of this walking game, Eric.'

It was a video of me waddling along the pavement being ridiculed by half the children in the neighbourhood. The girls must have been filming me on their mobile phones and then, just in case humiliating me in the street wasn't quite enough, they decided to do it over the internet too. The video had only been online a couple of hours and it already had nearly five thousand views.

I deleted the one on my timeline but the bloody thing was popping up everywhere. Every few minutes I'd receive another notification as one of my so called friends tagged me in. Even John and Mary had liked and shared it, and they've only been on Facebook since last Sunday.

Helen said, "I don't know why you're getting yourself so worked up Eric. You were like this when Sophie put up that photograph of you falling in the wheelie bin, but people have nearly forgotten about that already."

"That's right." Nodded Sophie. "Hardly anybody likes your arse anymore dad. No matter how many times I keep sharing it."

"Nearly forgotten about it?" I protested. "Hardly a day goes by without somebody getting in my taxi and mentioning that bloody picture. If it hadn't been for one of those girls remembering my backside yesterday, I probably would have gotten home with my dignity still intact."

Helen shook her head dismissively. "Well, I think you're worrying about nothing. You mark my words. All this will have been forgotten about by tea time."

Helen was wrong. By the time we'd finished our tea the video had over thirty thousand views, ten thousand likes, and had been shared one hundred and twenty eight times. Including once by my wife, and five times by my daughter.

Diary, I sometimes wonder why I even bloody bother.

Sunday 22nd June

Jumped on the scales before work. I was hoping the stress of being ridiculed over the internet and being chased home by a gang of feral children may have contributed towards me becoming a little slimmer, but frustratingly I've actually put on a pound?

How on Earth is that even possible? I tried again after having another wee, but even that didn't make any difference. It's no wonder people give up their diets so easily. Every time you think you're getting somewhere a pound of fat comes along and slaps you in the face again.

On the plus side the video of being me being bullied seems to have lost a little momentum. When I logged on

Facebook it had only amassed another fifteen thousand views, and been shared another eighty six times. If things carry on in this vein, the bloody thing might have been forgotten about by the time I retire.

Monday 23rd June

Since Helen and I fell out Carol has been sending me cryptic message after cryptic message alluding to their chat over lunch. I've been deleting and trying to ignore them, but she knows I hate the idea of them chatting away about me behind my back and has been taking great delight in trying to wind me up about it ever since.

The last straw came when I received a text that read, 'I can't believe you used to just roll off and go to sleep straight after sex, Eric. The least you should do is say thank you to the poor woman first.'

After that I decided I'd had enough. I text Carol I was on my way, jumped in the car, and sped round to her flat, fully intending to find out exactly what Helen had told her about me. Unfortunately Carol completely caught me by surprise by answering the door in her nightie, while holding a delicious looking slice of chocolate cake.

"Eric!" She screeched, sucking up some of the errant cream from her cake coated fingers, "I'm so glad you came. I knew you wouldn't be able to resist temptation forever."

I gulped loudly as I looked her up and down. “Are you talking about you, or the chocolate cake Carol?”

“Either one works for me Eric,” She purred. “Come on. Why don’t you try a little taste?” Then she launched herself towards me and began slobbering hungrily at my earlobe.

I couldn’t believe it. Not only was I being groped by Carol in full view of the street, but I was also trying to fend off her cake filled advances too.

The woman was like a bloody octopus. Every time I pulled her left hand away from my nipples, or my genitals, her right hand would suddenly pop up trying to force a bit of cake into my mouth. Carol was clearly trying to persuade me to come over to the dark side in more ways than one.

While there’s no denying Carol’s sexual allure, even if my penis had suddenly decided to break his vagina embargo and come out to play, I would have sent him quickly back inside with a flea in his ear. However, no matter how delicately Carol’s tongue nibbled against my neck, he just wasn’t interested. There wasn’t even a flicker.

“Carol, please. That's not why I’m here.”

“Yes, it is,” She said, rubbing her hips slowly against mine, “You just won’t admit it. Come on Eric, let yourself go.”

Mustering all my willpower I untangled myself from her wanton embrace and pushed her away. "No, it bloody isn't," I said firmly, "And for God's sake put some proper clothes on woman. You'll catch your death walking about like that."

Carol folded her arms and pouted at me like a scorned schoolgirl. "Well, you're no fun," she sighed, "If you're going to be like that you may as well come inside."

Being masterful wasn't something that came naturally to me but on this occasion I really didn't feel like I had a choice. Not only did I want make it clear to Carol that I just wasn't interested, but while Carol was molesting me a small crowd of onlookers had gathered on the pavement and I wanted to get her inside as quickly as possible.

Talk about embarrassing. As well as cheering us on, one boy even had the cheek to shout, "Go on mister. Give her one from me."

Once indoors and away from prying eyes, I sat Carol down and demanded she tell me everything she and my wife had talked about.

Diary, it was even worse than I thought. As I sat and listened to Carol reeling off the list of Helen's grievances, I think I actually let out a little sob.

According to Carol, my many faults include, being fat, being bald, snoring, farting too much, eating too noisily, eating with my mouth open, not cutting my toenails, making no effort with the children, making no effort with the neighbours, being unhealthily obsessed with the neighbour's cat, being unhealthily obsessed with the neighbour's cat's, cat shit, and not changing my underpants often enough.

Then, as if that wasn't enough, Helen told Carol that when, for the sake of our marriage she tried to put all my faults aside, and rekindle our sex life, I wasn't even interested. She thinks, because I've turned her down a couple of times, it's because I don't fancy her anymore?

While after seeing myself naked I could perfectly understand Helen not becoming a quivering wreck of sexual moistness whenever she saw me in my birthday suit, how on Earth could she think I've stopped wanting her? The woman must be stark staring bonkers. Every single day I look at my wife and thank the heavens for how lucky I am. Even if little Eric doesn't.

As I was trying to take it all in Carol went through to the kitchen and emerged again moments later, carrying a huge slice of cake. It was so big it was overlapping the sides of the plate. Carol handed it to me and joined me on the sofa. One hand snaking around my shoulder as the other patted me gently on the thigh. "Just in case you changed your mind," She said, gesturing towards the delicious looking triangular wedge of chocolate and cream. "You look like you need it."

Carol was right. I was so depressed right then I could have eaten a scabby horse if she'd had one in the fridge. I looked at the cake and then back at Carol. Two of my biggest weaknesses. Alright, it was mostly my own fault, but one way or another, they'd both contributed to the predicament I was in. If it hadn't been for both of them leading off the straight and narrow, I would have probably been home, back to my ideal weight, and making love to a wife with a full and proper erection. Instead, I was on Carol's sofa, wondering whether the chocolate tasted as good as it looked, and wondering how long it would be before Carol pounced on me again. Judging by how fast her hand was advancing up my leg it probably wouldn't be too long at all.

Carol shook her head and sighed. "You know, I'm sorry you had to hear all that Eric, I really am. I didn't want to have to tell you, but, well - you forced it out of me. I guess there are some women out there who don't realise how lucky they are." She leaned in closer and whispered seductively in my ear. "Not me though, lover. I don't care how dirty your underpants are. You can pop them in my Zanussi now if you like? It'll only take half an hour if I do them on a boil wash."

Diary, as I once more felt temptations fingers galloping towards my nether regions I came to a decision. It was a decision I've made many times before. The difference being this time I knew that I meant it. One way or another, I needed to get the good ship Eric back on course, and I was never going to do that while I was docking in Carol's choppy waters.

With a steely look in my eye and a newfound determination I yanked Carol's hand away from my groin, handed her back the plate, and calmly stood up.

“Anything wrong, Eric? You not eating your cake?”

“No Carol,” I said, “I will not be eating your cake. And what's more you will not be washing my Y fronts either. Contrary to popular belief they are not dirty, they’ve never been dirty, and even if they were, the last thing I’d be doing with them is putting them in your bloody Zanussi. Now if you’ll excuse me. It’s time I was getting home to my wife.”

Carol called after me as I strode purposely down the hallway. “You mean the wife who doesn't appreciate you, Eric? What exactly do you have to get home for?”

I paused. “Everything Carol. I have everything to get home for. I’m just sorry it took me so long to realise it.” Then I left, certain I would never eat cake or set foot in that flat ever again.

I may be bald, overweight and flaccid, but better that, than let Carol get me down to my underpants again. It's humiliating enough knowing she knows everything about me she does, without throwing a floppy little Eric into the mix too.

After leaving Carol’s I drove around for hours trying to get things straight in my head. Most of my apparent shortcomings were things Helen and Sophie took great delight in pointing out to me on a daily basis anyway, but as for the rest? Did Helen really believe I no longer fancied her? Did she really think I don’t change my underpants often enough? Did she really believe I was obsessed with the next door neighbour's cat?

Hercules may not be my favourite animal in the world, but I'd hardly say I was obsessed. Apart from when it has a poo in my garden, glares at me through the blinds, or helps itself to my bloody milk, I hardly ever give the fat ginger shitting machine a second thought.

By the time I arrived home it was already dark. I parked up outside and looked up towards the house. The blinds were closed, but inside I could see the light from the television and the silhouette of Helen pedalling away on the bike. Even in silhouette form she looked amazing. How could she possibly think any man, let alone me, could ever not want her?

I knew what I had to do. From now on there would be no more lies, no more excuses, If Helen and I were going to have any chance at all she needed to know everything.
Well, everything apart from what almost happened with Carol. I may be a complete idiot but I'm not bloody stupid. If Helen were to find out about Carol I wouldn't have to worry about little Eric not working anymore because Helen would have ripped him off and turned him into penis pate.

As I was still trying to figure it all out, next door's cat leapt up onto the bonnet. It wasn't a particularly warm night so it probably wanted to snuggle up against the warmth of the engine. As it settled itself down against the windscreen and began purring at me through half closed eyes, I thought about squirting it with the windscreen washers, but remembering Helen's words I decided to let it alone. I didn't even consider switching on the wipers when it started sticking its tongue out at me.

Cat obsessed indeed. As far as I'm concerned, nothing could be further from the truth.

By the time I plucked up the courage to go indoors, Sophie was sprawled out on the floor, engrossed in a movie, and Helen was fast asleep on the sofa. She looked so peaceful and contented I decided not to disturb her. Telling your wife you're limper than a wet lettuce is news that can probably wait until tomorrow.

Tuesday 24th June

Spent most of it tossing and turning as, in my head, I planned out the conversation I needed to have with Helen. Normally I like to play things by ear, but informing your wife you've become only half a man isn't really a conversation you can do off the cuff. "Do you fancy a cup of tea Helen? Oh, and by the way, I can't get an erection anymore. Do you want sugar with that?"

Then I decided to wait until tonight. Not only did I want to put it off for a little while longer, but Sophie was going to see Timothy after school and it'd give Helen and I a chance to talk without interruption. The last thing I need is my daughter overhearing little Eric isn't working properly. Knowing Sophie, she'd probably post up a status about it and tag me and her mother in.

My day at work was torturous. At times of stress my usual coping mechanism is to put away food like Homer Simpson at an all you can eat buffet. But because I'm determined to keep to my diet, the only food I took to work with me were an apple and a couple of bananas. Unfortunately, I was so stressed I'd gobbled them down before I'd even picked up my first fare. On the plus side, at least practically starving to death took my mind off my problems for a while. It's difficult to focus on other things when your stomach's growling at you like a pack of angry Alsatians.

All too soon, the day was over, and I was parked up outside the house. Hercules must have been waiting for my car to reappear because as soon as I switched off the engine he was back up on the bonnet again.

Honestly, you'd think if Ron insisted on owning cats, he'd at least install a cat flap so they could go inside when they wanted to escape the elements. It's no wonder the bloody animal is always doing its business in my garden. If Hercules is anything like me, as soon as he feels a bit of a chill in the air, he's probably going off like a fire extinguisher.

As Hercules and I sat inches apart, separated by only a thin sheet of glass, our eyes met, and I began to feel a sense of empathy for the animal. Maybe that cat and I were more similar than I cared to admit. Both old, both overweight, both with limited bladder control. I started the engine to give Hercules a few more minutes of warmth, and myself a little bit more thinking time, took a deep breath and then went inside.

When I'd finished explaining why I'd been so distant the last few weeks, Helen fell silent for a moment. Then she stood up, walked slowly towards me, and threw her arms around my waist. "Oh Eric," She said, burying her face in my chest. "Why on Earth didn't you just tell me?"

I said, "I don't know," and pulled her even closer. Her hair smelled of coconut. We both cried.
Diary, I really have been a complete and utter fool.

Wednesday 25th June

Woke up in the middle of the night, to find the duvet had been pulled away, and Helen was having a good rummage around inside my pyjama bottoms. I asked her what on Earth she thought she was doing?

Helen replied, "Well, I just thought if I caught it off guard, it might suddenly spring back to life."

I said, "I'm pretty sure it doesn't work like that Helen. You can't sneak up on the little guy and surprise him."

She said, "You never know. Go back to sleep and I'll give it another try."

I shook my head. "How am I expected to get back to sleep when I know you're going to be molesting me as soon as I nod off? Imagine how you'd feel if you woke up in the middle of the night to find me having a fiddle about underneath your nightie?"

Helen rolled her eyes, fell back on the bed, and pulled the duvet tightly around her shoulders. "Honestly Eric," She sighed, "you can be so melodramatic at times."

I didn't get much sleep after that. I spent the next few hours, listening to the sound of my stomach grumbling, and scrolling through Facebook.

So far the video of me being bullied by toddlers has received nearly seventy eight thousand views, and been shared just under five hundred times. Even the local vigilante group had shared it to their group to help show how crime ridden the streets have become.

I have to admit, I did feel a pang of guilt when I saw how many people were putting in orders for vigilante T shirts. But then thought, if nothing else, at least I'm providing a much needed boost to the local clothing economy. If anything, I've probably done the town a favour.

Once Sophie had left for school, Helen spent most of the morning on the internet, digesting everything she could find on the subject of impotency. I'm not sure what she expected to find but she was on there for hours. She was even making little notes on her phone so she could look them up again later.
When she switched off the computer, Helen pursed her lips, and nodded her head sagely, as though she were now an expert in the subject.

"Have you been to see the doctor yet?"

When I told her I hadn't, Helen immediately picked up the phone to make an appointment.

"It's no good putting these things off Eric," She said, as she scrolled through her phonebook. "Otherwise, you never know where it might lead."

I sighed, "Well, it certainly isn't going to get any floppier, if that's what's concerning you."

Helen rolled her eyes, "Don't be so flippant Eric. It says on here, your – you know, trouble, could be a symptom of a much more serious underlying medical condition."

I told her as he was often fine first thing in the morning, it was probably more psychological than anything else, but Helen insisted we make an appointment anyway. "Better to be safe than sorry," She said. "Oh, and don't worry, I'll make sure I ask for a man."

Say what you like about my wife, but she certainly isn't one to let the grass grow under her feet.

For lunch I made us both some Mackerel on toast, then we sat down to watch Loose Women together.

During the first advert break Helen turned toward me. "You're sure it isn't me, then?" She asked, looking up at me with the crooked half smile she always wears when she's feeling slightly nervous.

I took hold of her hand and gave it a squeeze. "Of course it isn't you," I said. "I want you more than I ever did."

"Really?"

"Yes, really. If a naked Kylie Minogue walked in here and asked me to join her in a horizontal locomotion it wouldn't make a blind bit of difference. It's me that's the problem. Not you. Well, it's not even me really," I said, nodding towards my zipper, "It's that little shit down there."

Helen snuggled herself against me. "He always did have a mind of his own."

As we listened to Janet Street Porter, Martine McCutcheon, and Samantha Fox discussing how the Syrian crisis could be solved if everyone could just learn how to get along better, I thought about asking Helen if she still fancied me. Somehow though, as I felt Carol's fingers absently stroking my shirt covered paunch, it just didn't seem necessary.

While there was no denying our sex life had dwindled away to nothing over the last twelve months, all I could sense from Helen right then, was warmth, love and affection. I just hoped she could sense it back.

Just before bed I received a text from Carol saying she couldn't believe that I'd walked out on her a second time, but swore that it wouldn't be happening again.

I texted back saying, too bloody right it wouldn't be, because I had no intention of ever going round to her place again. She replied, 'Well, actually Eric. I meant it as more of a threat than a promise.
I replied back, 'Oh, sorry, my mistake,' then turned off my phone.

Thursday 26th June

Doctors

Another restless night's sleep. Not only did I have Carol, and my visit to the doctors playing on my mind, but Andrew is performing at The Wheatsheaf on Saturday so he was practising in the shed until well after dark. The music wasn't too bad, but it didn't help that most of the cats and dogs in the street were trying to outdo him by joining in with the chorus.

I was going to go and ask him to keep it down, but Ron beat me to it. We heard his bedroom window slam open, followed by, "Shut the fuck up will you. Some of us have got work in the morning."

After that, everything went quiet. Even the cats and dogs didn't bother to argue.

When I did eventually manage to fall asleep, I dreamt Carol was my GP. I complained that we'd specifically asked to see a male doctor but the receptionist told us

Carol was the only person available, and she was a specialist in medical conditions emanating below the waistline.

I was all for walking out, but Helen told me to stop being so pathetic and dragged me through to the examination room.
Once inside Carol insisted I strip off completely. As I stood with my legs apart, carefully holding my stomach out of the way, she then proceeded to give little Eric a thorough, and I mean thorough, examination.

Diary, it was horrible. With my wife looking on, Doctor Carol was lifting and pulling, and twisting and turning, then when I dared to look down I was horrified to discover she'd turned little Eric into a balloon animal dog. I couldn't believe it. She'd even used my testicles as a couple of floppy ears.

When I questioned her credentials as a legitimate doctor, a grinning Carol said, "Don't worry, Mr Baxter. We'll soon have the little guy sorted." Then she pulled a pin from the top pocket of her white coat and burst little Eric by stabbing him in the left ear.

It isn't often that I wake up in a cold sweat, frantically wiping imaginary exploded testicle skin off my face, but that was one of those moments.

Compared to my dream, the visit to the doctors was much less scary than I imagined. Before being called in, Helen asked if I'd prefer her to stay in the waiting room. I had no intention of telling the doctor anything about

Carol but I still thought it was best I went in alone. There are some things a man just doesn't want his wife to see or hear, no matter how long they've been married.

The GP I saw was Doctor Malik. A short, kindly man, with glasses and thinning silver hair. He listened, nodding occasionally, as I told him all about little Eric.

When I'd finished, he took my blood pressure, listened to my heartbeat, and then took some blood.

He said I'd done the right thing going to see him. He explained how an erectile dysfunction was sometimes a signifier of other illnesses. Then he asked me step behind the screen and get undressed.

As I stood unbuckling my belt, I began to ask the questions most men ask themselves in the same situation. Did the doctor want me to remove my trousers completely or would it be acceptable to leave them round my ankles? Did he actually want me on the couch or would it be alright if I just bent over? I tried various positions, but none of them seemed right. I settled for lying back with my trousers and underpants completely off, trying not to look as awkward and uncomfortable as I felt inside. When the examination was over I got dressed and re-joined the doctor.

"Well, everything seems fine," He said, as he keyed my information into his computer. "Your blood pressure is marginally on the high side, and I'm not exactly happy about your weight, but then I'm sure you know that already."

He then depressingly listed a range of diseases associated with obesity almost as long as my waistline.

"But overall," He continued, "For your age and your size, you appear to be quite healthy. Though from the symptoms you describe I'm almost certain this isn't a physical issue."

To say I was relieved would be an understatement. Outwardly I managed to remain calm, but inside I leapt out of the chair and planted a very wet kiss slap bang in the middle of the doctor's forehead.

Even though I knew the reasons behind my problem were the guilt, the lies, the deceit, and the ever present shadow of Carol looming large on the horizon, it was nice to have my diagnosis confirmed by someone other than Google.

Dr Malik leaned towards me and smiled. "Tell me, Mr Baxter, has there been anything troubling you lately? Anything you've been concerned about?"

Diary, I only meant to disclose the select highlights, but once I started I couldn't stop. It was like asking the question had turned on a tap and everything just came gushing forth.

I told him about the rumour I'd accidentally started to try and boost business at work. I told him of my constant battle with food and my failed attempts at weight loss. I told him how it'd been so long since my wife and I had made love I was worried I'd forgotten how to do it. I told him about next door's cat and his overly proficient bottom. I told him about my daughter and the ginger gorilla, I even told him about the video of me being ridiculed by hordes of evil children as I walked along the street. Then I told him about Carol. I really did tell him everything.

When I'd finished, the doctor removed his glasses, and lightly shook his head. "Extraordinary," He said. "Absolutely extraordinary."

I left the surgery clutching a diet sheet, the name and address of a local psychiatrist and a prescription for Viagra. Dr Malik said it was a toss of a coin as to which one he felt I needed the most.

Friday 27th June

Everything was pretty much back to normal today. I woke up to the sound of my stomach grumbling and then spent the rest of the day thinking about food. This turning over a new leaf business is all well and good, but it doesn't half make you bloody hungry.

What surprised me most was how resolute I was in the face of temptation. Despite driving past countless fast food places, restaurants, and fish and chip shops, I didn't think about stopping once. Although I did slow to a leisurely crawl with the windows wound down a couple of times.

Helen was back to her old self too. She'd obviously decided I'd been mollycoddled enough and was having a go at the tough love route. When I asked her to pass me the milk during breakfast, she said, "Get it yourself you lazy sod, you're not a bloody invalid."

Thinking about little Eric I almost joked, well actually, I'm not completely able bodied, but then thought better of it. Especially with Sophie sitting opposite. That girl's mind is so sharp I'm surprised she doesn't cut herself thinking.

While out on an airport run, I thought I'd stop off at a chemist in Stockport to pick up my prescription. Helen said I should have done it yesterday, but there's no way I was getting this prescription filled locally. I don't even like the local Chemists knowing I suffer from corns, or the occasional verruca. I certainly didn't want them knowing I suffer from erection problems too. Imagine trying to make small talk if they ever got in my cab? I may not have much left in the way of pride, but the little bit I do still have, I'd like to hang on to.

As is usually the case these days, every chemist shop I called in to had a young woman serving behind the counter. Eight shops I visited altogether and there wasn't any sign of a man in any of them. It's no wonder teenage pregnancy is on the increase. All the teenage boys are probably too embarrassed to buy a condom.

After driving round for an hour, getting more and more frustrated, I resolved to go in the next chemist I came to, no matter who was serving. Unfortunately, after striding purposely towards the smiling, petite, blonde girl, clutching my prescription, I completely lost my nerve, and came away with a box of plasters and a packet of paracetamol.

Diary, it seems strange, part of me was actually feeling relieved. Although I was really looking forward to being with Helen again, I couldn't help wondering what would happen if it all went wrong? You read horror stories about it in the papers all the time. Men waddling into the A & E department, wearing loose fitting trousers, and sporting a three day old erection. If that was going to happen to anyone you could guarantee it would be me. Or what if I took the pill and absolutely nothing happened? What use would I be to anybody then?

Helen was still at work when I arrived home. I sent her a text telling her I was sorry, but I hadn't had time to collect the prescription. She replied, 'There's no rush Eric,' followed by a smiley face and a kiss.

I really don't know what I've done to deserve that woman. I must have been a saint in a previous life, because I certainly haven't done anything to merit being with her in this one.
As I was taking my shoes off in the hall, I heard muffled voices coming from upstairs. My first thought was that Andrew was in the bath with Abigail again. I was about to shout up and tell them to make sure they rinsed out the sponge this time, when I realised the voices were actually coming from Sophie's room. Not only that, diary, but one of the voices was most definitely male.

I couldn't believe it. Even though I'd strictly forbidden it, my daughter had clearly gone against my wishes and invited Timothy, the six foot ginger gorilla, up to her bedroom. Assuming the worst, I galloped up the stairs with all sorts of horrifying images going through my mind. And it didn't help allay my fears when I heard the following exchange take place as I reached the top landing.

Sophie: "Do you like it?"

Timothy: "Sophie, it looks amazing."

Sophie: "Hang on. I'll take these clothes off so you can see it properly."

Upon hearing that I threw open the bedroom door, fully expecting to find a couple of half-naked teenagers making out on the top of Sophie's Manchester United duvet set. But much to my relief there was only my daughter removing her blue denim jacket from around the shoulders of her wonky eyed Wayne Rooney cardboard cut-out.

"Dad, what are you doing?" She yelled. "You know you're not allowed in here."

I looked around the room and blinked several times, as I tried to figure out where his voice had been coming from. "Sorry, I just thought…where's Timothy?"

"Hey, Mr Baxter."

I looked down, and in the palm of Sophie's hand was Timothy’s gormless grinning face glaring back at me from the screen of her mobile phone. He waved at me, and I waved back.

“I don’t believe you dad,” Said Sophie, ushering me out of the room. “I don’t get any privacy in this house. Can’t we even face time now without you sticking your nose in?”

After apologising to my daughter and reluctantly promising to fit a lock to her door, I headed back downstairs. I’ve got a feeling I’ll be apologising for this one for a very long time.

Saturday 28th June

Gig night.

After breakfast (Two Weetabix and a banana), I spent the morning driving around, trying to find a chemist with a male assistant. By the time I arrived home, I had amassed three jars of Vaseline, two combs, four packets of Ibuprofen, a hair band, a pair of surgical stockings, but still no prescription.

When I told Helen, I still hadn’t had a chance to collect it, she smiled sympathetically, told me there was no rush, and then snatched the prescription out of my hand. “I’ll pick it up myself,” She said.

I can only hope there isn't anyone we know in the shop when she goes to collect it.

Diary, although I haven't even started the doctor's diet plan, whatever I've been doing recently, it definitely seems to be working. As I was getting ready for tonight I jumped on the scales, and was amazed to discover I now weigh only 259lbs. That means I've lost nearly half a stone in under a fortnight. It may be only one pound less than when I started this bloody diet, but after recent events, it felt like a minor miracle.

Helen was so pleased when I told her, she threw her arms around my neck, and kissed me on the cheek. "Well done, Eric," She said. "I knew you could do it."

A furrowed browed Sophie, was a lot more begrudging with her praise. "Yes, well done dad." She said, whilst repeatedly stepping on and off the scales to make sure they were still working properly.

It might not sound like much, but I couldn't detect a hint of sarcasm in her voice. At one point, I almost thought she was going to break out into a smile.

We arrived at The Wheatsheaf just before seven. Andrew wasn't due on stage until later, but we had to pick Melody up on the way, and Sophie insisted we all arrive early so we could soak in the atmosphere.

When we got there, Andrew grabbed his guitar, and said he was going to find Abigail. We knew we were unlikely to see him again until he performed, so before he disappeared, we all took the opportunity to wish him luck.

Sophie, who normally loathes public shows of affection, once again surprised everyone by throwing her arms around him and telling him to break a leg. If that had been me she would have probably meant it. A teary eyed Helen, unnecessarily straightened the collar of our son's T shirt, and kissed him on the cheek. Then Andrew and I shook hands. It was the first handshake between father and son. He knew how proud I was of him.

Diary, even though we were early the place was absolutely packed. Sitting on the floor near the stage area were a few other young teenage girls. No sooner had we found a table than Sophie and Melody scurried off to join them, leaving Helen and me to fend for ourselves.

I went off to get some drinks and refreshments. A large glass of red for Helen, half a bitter shandy for me, orange juice and crisps for the girls.

All I'd had to eat since breakfast was spinach, tomatoes, and an omelette, so I treated myself to a packet of cheese and onion. I'd been so good lately I felt I deserved a treat, and the last thing people wanted to hear during the performance was my stomach grumbling. If anything, I was actually eating the crisps for the audience's benefit rather than my own.

When I got back, Sophie and Melody came galloping back to our table, knocked back their drinks, grabbed their crisps, and then buggered off again. I didn't even get a thank you.

Helen said. "When did Andrew turn into Justin Bieber?"

I said, "There is another act on before Andrew. Maybe everybody's come to see them?"

Helen gestured towards the girls. "I shouldn't think so. I can't imagine any of that lot being interested in a middle aged folk singer who plays the ukulele." She took a sip of her wine. "Mind you, Andrew does have that vampire look girls seem to go for these days."

I had to agree. If Andrew's skin was any pastier he'd probably turn see-through. Rather than being a vampire, I put it down to him not getting enough iron in his diet, and spending too much time canoodling in the shed with Abigail.
Helen sat up in her seat, and began looking over my shoulder towards the far side of the room. "Is that who I think it is?" She said, craning her neck for a better view.

I followed the direction of Helen's eyes and my heart sank. Standing at the far side of the room, drinks in hand, and waving frantically in our direction, were Carol and Harry. I groaned inwardly. That woman is proving even harder to get rid of than both my double chins.

I'd no idea what they were doing there together, but they'd clearly made the effort to dress up for the evening. Harry was wearing a navy blue pinstripe suit, accompanied by a bright red dickie bow. Carol had poured herself into a figure hugging blue strapless dress, bulging in all the right places, as well as the wrong ones, and a pair of the highest heels I've ever seen. How she managed to remain upright is a mystery. If she hadn't been using Harry's arm as a counterbalance to her breasts, she'd likely have toppled over.

"Helen. Eric." Screeched Carol. "You got room for a little one in there?" Then, without waiting to be asked, she squeezed past my chair towards the empty seat. Deliberately clanking me on the side of the head with her glass as she went. Harry sat down opposite her and put down his coffee. Any questions I may have had as to whether Carol was there to torment me or not, were answered, when I felt her fingers latch onto my thigh beneath the table and give it a squeeze.

Helen said, "I didn't know you two were coming tonight?"

Carol nodded. "I wouldn't have missed it for the world. As soon as I saw it advertised on Facebook, I rushed off to buy a couple of tickets. If that son of yours is anything like this one here," She said, gesturing towards me, "He'll have the girls eating out of his hand in no time."

Helen pointed at Harry and Carol in turn. "Oh, does that mean you two are together then?"

Carol tilted her head and raised her eyebrows. "Well, normally I like my men with a lot more meat on them," She said, as she again grabbed my thigh beneath the table. "But never say never, eh, Harry? I needed a chaperone for the evening and Harry here was good enough to volunteer."

Taking his cue, Harry stood up and did an exaggerated bow. Bending forward from the waist and flamboyantly swinging his right arm across his chest. "At your service, m'lady."

"Oh, how very gallant," Said Helen, admiringly. "Why can't you be more like that Eric?"

I didn't reply. Like a member of river dance, I was too busy trying to remain motionless from the waist up, while fending off Carol's hand beneath the table. I coughed, and subtly moved my chair backwards a little. Not quite out of harm's reach, but far enough away to make it difficult for her.

Helen said, "You know, you could do a lot worse for yourself than Harry, Carol. There aren't that many gentlemen left in the world."

Carol glanced in my direction. "You don't have to tell me. Most of the men I've met recently are just plain cowardly."

She was obviously referring to me, but even if my wife hadn't been there I'd have hardly been in a position to argue. My recent behaviour had been so yellow bellied, even Scooby Doo and Shaggy would've been too ashamed to be seen with me. Carol then changed her demeanour, and turned toward Harry. "Still, out with the old, and in with the decrepit." She said, taking a large swig of her wine. "Who knows what might happen once I've got a few more of these inside me."

As Helen and Carol began nattering away, a beaming Harry leant towards me, and patted his chest pocket. "Good job I brought my sheath," He whispered. "I reckon I'm in there."

I almost choked on my shandy. "Didn't you hear what she just said?"

Harry nodded. "Once she's pissed I'm in with a chance. Sounds like I'm on a promise to me."

I shook my head. "You dirty old git. You're old enough to be her dad."

Harry scoffed, and straightened his shoulders, "There's a many a good tune played on an old fiddle, Eric. Even if the bow has been gathering dust in my trousers for the last fifteen years."

I had to admire his optimism. Even being insulted didn't seem to put him off. Although he was probably too distracted by Carol's breasts, as they fought to break free from her dress, to focus on anything else. I was finding them pretty distracting myself. Every time Carol made a sudden movement they looked like they were about to spill out all over the table.

Harry tore his eyes away and jumped to his feet. "Right, I better get some more drinks. Same again, Carol? Actually…never mind…I'll just bring a bottle."

The first act was on soon so I went with him. When we got back, I made sure I got to the table first and casually sat down in Harry's chair. Helen smiled, and patted me on the hand. She obviously thought I'd moved so I could be closer to her.

While that was partly true, it was mostly so Carol wouldn't be able to reach me with her hand again. The last thing I wanted was Carol groping me underneath the table while I was trying to listen to Andrew. Harry didn't seem to mind. He plonked himself down next to Carol and filled her glass to the brim. "Plenty more where that came from," he said."

The folk singer was much better than I expected. A tall bearded man walked on stage, carrying his ukulele, and sporting a huge bushy beard that covered half his face, and hung down to his midriff. As with most folk singers I had absolutely no idea what he was singing about but it certainly sounded good.

He sung one song about the moon, a couple of songs about a girl called Rosie, and I couldn't be sure, but I think the last one was about a unicorn. Whatever the lyrics, the music was certainly infectious. Everybody was clapping their hands, tapping their feet, and when I looked to the foot of the stage, even Sophie and Melody were joining in.

The only people in the room who didn't get involved were Harry and Carol. Throughout the set they were flirting with each other like a couple of teenagers. It was painfully obvious Carol was only doing it to make me jealous, but poor old Harry didn't know that.

Carol was playing with his hair, whispering in his ear, and giggling hysterically at all his jokes. Diary, I've known Harry for over ten years and he's never been that funny. He's certainly never made me laugh so hard that wine spurted out of my nostrils.

I could see Helen was losing her patience too. Under normal circumstances she probably would have thought it amusing, but this was our son's first ever performance. Judging by how fast the vein was throbbing in her temple, amused was the last thing Helen was. She kept jabbing me on the shoulder and gesturing towards them. She obviously wanted me to say or do something, but short of throwing a bucket of water over the pair of them, I had no idea what. Glaring sternly across the table certainly wasn't having an effect.

Next on stage was Andrew. I thought he was singing alone, so it was quite a surprise when Abigail joined him too. Not that she added much. Aside from looking pretty, all she really did was roll her head from side to side, shaking her tambourine.

Diary, I must admit, I thought it was going to be difficult for our son to follow the first act but I needn't have worried. He started off by singing a rip roaring version of '*Wonderwall*' by 'Oasis,' that literally had the whole room rocking. Then he calmed everybody down again with a haunting rendition of '*Hallelujah,*' by 'Jeff Buckley.'

It was slightly unsettling having Carol and Harry groping each other in my peripheral vision, but despite that, I was really enjoying it. At least I was until Andrew started singing, '*Hit the Road Jack,'* and Carol suddenly climbed onto Harry's lap and stuck her tongue halfway down his throat.

A couple of days ago, Carol was trying to get in my pants, and now she was straddling a pensioner and sucking his face off. I didn't know whether to be relieved or insulted. If Harry wore false teeth I hoped he was using a strong adhesive. I doubt even a tube of superglue would have held them in place under the strength of Carol's onslaught. Their slobbering was making so much noise everybody in the room turned towards us to see what the commotion was.

People were tutting and shaking their heads, while Sophie, Melody and the rest of the girls, were booing and throwing crisps across the room.

It was when Andrew became so distracted, he began to stumble over his words, I finally snapped. Or at least I would have done if Helen hadn't beaten me to it. As soon as she realised Andrew was struggling, my wife grabbed her glass of wine, and threw it all over Carol. "Will you two kindly give it a rest," She yelled. "In case you hadn't noticed, my son is trying to bloody sing up there."

As the room fell silent, Carol, slowly climbed off Harry's lap, and stood with her arms outstretched. You wouldn't think a glass of wine could cause such a mess, but Carol was drenched. It was all over her arms, her clothes, her hair, and dripping down into her cleavage.

Open mouthed, she turned towards me, and looked herself up and down. “Are you just going to sit there and let your wife speak to me like that, Eric?”

To show Carol exactly where my allegiance lay, I took my wife's hand. “Just go home Carol,” I said. “I think you've embarrassed everyone enough for one night.”

Carol stared at me across the table. I really did think she was going to blow my world apart. After everything that’d happened, I certainly wouldn't have blamed her if she had. However, all she did was grab Harry by the hand and pull him to his feet. “Come on you, we’re leaving,” She said, sticking her chest out in a show of defiance. “No point staying where we’re not wanted anymore.”

Ignoring the clapping and cheering, Carol and Harry linked arms and walked proudly towards the door. Or as proudly as they could walk with Harry bent awkwardly from the waist, as he tried to hide his erection.

When they reached the exit, Carol paused and looked towards me. The rest of the room faded into the background, and for a brief moment, Carol and I were the only two people there. No words were needed. She knew I wished her well. Then they were gone.

Once everything had settled down, Andrew was allowed to continue. He followed up his first three songs with

‘*Knockin on Heaven’s Door*’ by ‘Bob Dylan.’ ‘*Free Fallin*’ by Tom Petty. Then he finished off the evening with ‘*Brown Eyed Girl*’ by ‘Van Morrison.’ Judging by the goofy look on her face, the last song was obviously meant for Abigail. Strange really. Up until then, I always thought her eyes were green.

When he’d finished his set the audience rose as one and gave him a huge round of applause. Not quite as rapturous as the one Carol and Harry got when they left, but still pretty damned good.

As everyone joined us at the table, I apologised for the behaviour of my work colleagues. Andrew shook his head and told me not to worry about it. He then asked me what I thought of his performance.

Diary, I don't know whether it was the relief of knowing Carol wouldn’t be troubling me again, or because I was so proud. For the first time since he was a young boy I threw my arms around my son and held him. Then, because I could see Helen’s eyes welling up again, I pulled her into the melee too. The only person who didn’t join in was Sophie. “I am not hugging you in public, dad,” She said, slowly backing away. “People might think we’re related.”

It’s not often I put my foot down with my daughter, but this was one such occasion. I drew in my stomach to give myself a bit more cuddle room and held out my hand. Sophie didn’t take much convincing. As I felt my daughter relax against me, I closed my eyes and pulled my family even closer. I really am a very lucky man.

Andrew, ever the gentleman, was staying to walk Abigail home, so the rest of us decided to call it a night. Outside, I could see Harry's taxi further down the road. Judging by the steamed up windows and how fast the car was rocking they'd clearly decided to carry on where they left off in the pub. I only hope Harry knows what he's doing. I know for a fact it isn't that long since he had his suspension done.

We took Melody home, and arrived back at ours around eleven. As I parked up I noticed Hercules wasn't waiting for my car to arrive. I assumed he'd be in the back garden making full use of the toilet facilities, but there was no sign of him anywhere. I filled a saucer with milk and left it next to the back door. If I was going to be washing his pee off the shed in the morning I might as well make sure it was semi-skimmed.

Helen and Sophie joined me and asked me what I was doing. When I told them they both looked at me as though I'd just sprouted a second head.

Sophie said, "You're losing weight, and now you're feeding the neighbour's cat? Who are you and what have you done with my father?"

Helen said, "Not forgetting hugging his children. What's gotten into you tonight, Eric?"

I smiled. "Nothing got into me. I'm just in a good mood, that's all." And all things considered – it was true, I really was.

Just then Hercules appeared from the side of the house. We stood silently watching him until he'd emptied the saucer, then I picked him and scratched him behind the ear.

Sophie shook her head in bewilderment. "I'm sorry, but this is just too weird. I'm going to bed."

Helen and I went back inside, made ourselves a coffee, and switched on the television. As I was flicking through the channels, Helen asked how long I thought it'd be before Sophie fell asleep.

When I asked why, she looked at me curiously, grabbed her purse from the coffee table, and pulled out a prescription bag.

I immediately knew what it was. "When on Earth did you have a chance to go and get that?" I asked.

Helen said, "This afternoon. Well, you didn't really think it took nearly an hour to nip out and get a paper did you?"

I took the bag from her and pulled it open. Inside was a small plastic compartment containing a tiny blue pill.
I said, "You only get one? What happens if we want to have another go?"

Helen said. "It doesn't work like that. One pill lasts quite a few hours, apparently. Which will be an improvement because you usually only last a few minutes."

We both laughed. I was feeling quite nervous, so it was nice to break the ice a little.

Unfortunately, any plans we'd had for a night of unbridled passion we're soon scuppered when we read the leaflet and discovered I needed to take the pill at least an hour before any sexual activity. It was already half past eleven. I could barely keep my eyes open as it was. If little Eric was going to be primed and ready for action I at least wanted to be conscious while it was happening.

Helen sighed, "Don't worry. There's always tomorrow. I suppose we could just go to bed and…cuddle?"

I kissed my wife on the cheek. "That'll be really good."

Helen sat up and looked at me seriously. "But you will be putting that bloody cat back outside first, won't you Eric?"

I carried Hercules out to the back garden, and locked the back door. Then I took hold of Helen's hand and we headed up to bed.

Printed in Great Britain
by Amazon